SILENT KNIGHT

A HIRAM KANE ORIGIN STORY: A HIRAM KANE ACTION THRILLER

STEVEN MOORE

CONDOR PUBLISHING

SIGN UP?

SIGN UP for my bi-weekly spam-free newsletter to keep up with all my new releases and future promotions, not to mention your chance to win signed copies.

Just type this link into your web browser:

www.subscribepage.com/stevenmooreauthor

PROLOGUE

GONE ROGUE

Secret Cave System, Shropshire, England January 5th, 1308

"But we can not do that. We must not. It is not right."

Brother Deane de Tourville stood up from his haunches, keeping his head down beneath the low stone ceiling of the natural cave. He'd been uncomfortable about what they were doing from the very first mention of it, but as the youngest member of their order, he hadn't yet summoned the courage to speak up. But now he had to. It was simple. They had to turn themselves in to the King's Guards.

"But what choice do we have, Brother Tourville?" asked his mentor, James de Somervila. De Somervila was a big, battle-hardened man whose nose had been broken so many times it was little more than a gnarled lump of flesh. Though his voice was strong and firm, he had sympathy for the younger man's concerns. But sympathy might just get them killed. "If we do not stay hidden here now, Deane, we will be hunted down and captured, and then we will be tortured. After that, the King's bastards will burn us at the stake. I will not allow that to happen to you, my friend, especially after everything we have done in service to our God, our King and our country. I can not accept that, Brother Deane. I will not accept that."

Deane de Tourville knew his elder was right. He had always looked up to his mentor and leader, James de Somervila. The man had shown him the way of the Templar code ever since he had been ordained a Knight almost a decade ago, and his courage and guidance had been an inspiration to him over the last ten years of service. He trusted him with his life. But now? After narrowly escaping the murderous clutches of King Edward's men and seeking sanctuary in these caves? Deane knew he would have to trust in Brother James again.

The six Templar Knights gathered there in the secret caves beneath a field in Shropshire in western England were no ordinary Knights Templar. They had served the cause as bravely and vigilantly as any Knight, and many of their order had given everything to the Crusades, most of them making the ultimate sacrifice by paying with their lives. That of course was expected of all Templars; to die in service of God was to die a noble death.

And yet, they had returned home to England from those Crusades in the Holy Land enlightened. Not everything was as clear cut as they had been led to believe before they left from Nottingham all those years ago. Yes, they were God-fearing Christians. But they had also learned many things on their travels, and from many different people. And yes, some Templars had developed new beliefs that were in direct contradiction to what most of their Templar brethren believed.

Would they go directly against the Church for those new-found philosophies? Probably not.

But would they give up their lives for them? The answer to that was a definitive no.

These men knew they were innocent of the charges of heresy thrown at them by King Philip IV of France and above him, Pope Clement. But thousands of their number had been tracked and arrested for those charges, many already murdered, others being tortured into confessions on a daily basis. Thus, they had fled, gone rogue, and had made their way to this secret cave system in Shropshire, where they were prepared to wait for however long it took for the dust to clear and the accusations of heretic treachery to be dropped.

It had only been a week, however, and some of their number were growing impatient. One of those struggling was the youngest, Deane de Tourville. He sat down, leaning his broad back against the cave wall. Despite the icy conditions outside, the heat from their bodies and the oil lamps dotted around the cave kept them warm. Snow had been falling for days now, which at least helped to keep the entrance to the subterranean labyrinth hidden. For now.

They couldn't stay here forever. Very soon, Deane knew they would have to leave this place, head further afield and either flee abroad or find somewhere more permanent to live on the edges of society in Britain. But Deane didn't want to be on the run for the rest of his life. He was twenty-seven. He was officially a free man, with only the warped opinions of a few men declaring otherwise. While those corrupted men held power, the outcast Templars were not safe. And right now, Brother Deane de Tourville did not feel free at all.

Five miles away on a lonely country lane, thirteen horseman made their way cautiously north towards Caynton from Berkeley Castle. Among them were a dozen members of King Edward's Royal Guard. Strong men, skilled with weapons and prepared to use them to carry out their master's bidding.

Though he wore only the worn out robes of a peasant, the other man among them was no such thing. Approaching sixty, he was old for a Knight, his white hair hidden beneath a hood. But his age did not dull his mind, nor did it dull his greed.

He had left his magnificent Templar sword behind. He wouldn't need it. The equally ornate and equally lethal dagger he did bring along however would soon be slid from its leather scabbard. At its tip would be his heretic former Templar brother, James de Somervila.

CLOSING IN

The rogue Knights had slept fitfully for several hours when Brother Deane returned from his overnight lookout duty. He was freezing cold but, uncomplaining, he sat as close to the fire pit as he could. Others among them stirred, and soon all six men sat up, stretching the aches from their weary bones and longing for the day they no longer needed to hide beneath the frozen ground like a heard of hibernating mammals.

Brother Daren de Hassall took a long swig of beer from his hefty tankard and smacked his lips. His dark eyes scanned the group of his brothers. He appraised each of them one after another, exchanging with the older of them knowing glances. Finally his eyes rested on the recently returned youngest of them all, Deane de Tourville.

"You know they will come for us, Brother Deane.

It is just a matter of time. We are only six strong. But we must be ready." He cuffed frothy beer from his lips with the sleeve of his tunic. "When they come, and you can be sure they are coming, we must fight them unto death."

Brother Hassall was not the biggest of the Brothers gathered in the cave – he was tall but lean – yet without doubt he was the most feared when it came to fighting. His weathered face bore more scars than his scalp had hairs, and if he added what remained of both his ears together he could just about claim he had one. His fearsome reputation had been sealed some seventeen years ago, on a windswept coast during the siege of Acre a hundred miles north of Jerusalem. Daren had been cornered by a gang of four Mamluk warriors, forced to the edge of the rocky shoreline against which crashed wild Mediterranean waves. He had fought them off, killing them all with vicious yet skilled swings of his mighty blade. He had lost a hand and most of an arm for his troubles, but he laughed it off, telling anyone who would listen that God had seen fit to bless him with a spare.

"So I ask you, young Deane," said Daren de Hassall, "are you ready to fight?"

Deane stood again, keeping his back as straight as possible in the confines of the cave. "Yes, Brother Daren," Deane said, and took a deep solidifying breath. "I am ready."

"As am I," declared Nickolas de Thackere.

"And I," growled Davide de Berens.

John d'Opton, however, did not speak. He did not need to. A mere tip of his broad forehead told them everything they needed to know about his willingness to preserve their dignity, despite whatever forces they faced.

They had once sworn an oath, and the words — words that meant more to each and every one of them, more even than their own lives — they repeated together now, led by James de Somervila.

"I swear that I will defend by my words, arms, and every possible means..." he said, and the others repeated... "even with the loss of my own life, the mysteries and articles of the Faith, the Seven Sacraments, the Symbols of the Apostles and of Saint Athanasius, the Old and New Testaments with the explanations of the Holy Fathers approved by the Church, the unity of the Divine Nature and the Trinity of Persons in God, the virginity of the Virgin Mary before, during and after the parturition."

He paused, nodding with pride at the intensity with which his brothers repeated the oath. He continued, as did they.

"I promise obedience to the Grand Master of the Order according to the statutes of our Blessed Father Bernard. I will engage in combat on foreign lands whenever it is necessary. I will never flee from the infidels, even should I be alone. I will observe perpetual chastity.

"I will assist with my words, arms, and actions religious persons, principally the abbots and religious of the Cistercian Order, as our brethren and special friends with whom we have a perpetual association."

He stopped again. He shared a nod and the hint of a smile with each of his friends in that cave. They were more than friends. They were Brothers, not just in the name of the Order, but after all they had experienced, and of the experiences to come. They had become — and would always be — Brothers sealed in blood.

"I voluntarily swear before God and His Holy Gospel that I will keep all these commitments." Finally, he added, "And the commitments to come."

Each man raised his tankard and downed the remnants of the warm, stale beer. All bar none of them felt invincible surrounded by such loyal, courageous men. There was not a treacherous bone among them, and each knew all the others would lay down their lives for him if they were simply asked.

A mile away, the horses moved quicker across the rock-solid ground. The trotting became a gallop, and as the gallop became a flat out charge, the frosty earth beneath them shook under the weight of their pounding hooves. Despite the frigid air, beads of the horses' sweat flew from their necks and flanks, the very first rays of dawn glistening in every hard-earned drop.

At the rear of the convoy, the peasant-robed man clutched his reins tight. His heart raced, both from the exertion of the relentless ride north and the imminent, inevitable result. There was no doubt in his mind that what he had done was right. He had no choice. He was a man of God, and those who betrayed God deserved to face His punishment. That their punishment would likely be a public flogging, followed by torture, and finally being burnt alive at the stake on charges of heresy, was of no concern to him. It was a just punishment, for there was no greater crime than swaying from the word of the one Almighty God. They were blasphemers, pure and simple. There had even been rumours of devil worshipping. It mattered little. His decision to betray them was easy. It was made even easier due to the purse of gold coins he'd been promised.

He had been one of their order. He knew what they believed in. He had let himself be strayed by it too for a while... It was seductive. Impressive in many ways. But he had returned from his exploits in the Holy Land to stand once more by God's side...

Especially when God's servant King Edward was paying so well.

Brother Davide de Berens slapped young Brother Tourville on the back and made his way out of that part of the cave system. Next, he eased along the natural passageway towards the hidden entrance. The sun would soon be up, which meant one of them needed to be alert and on duty at all times. They did not expect trouble. Not yet. Nobody knew where they were, and they had recently learned that the only person who did know about the caves had been killed in a riding accident several weeks before. They were safe for now. But you could never be too careful, for treachery was a sin often worth its weight in coin.

Brother de Berens edged his way up through the narrow stone tunnel that led into the caves, then shielded his eyes against dawn's glow as he slipped his head through the hole to the outside world, which was nothing larger than the entrance to a badger's lair. He grinned as he thought of Brother Hassall's long frame getting wedged in the gap. When he hauled himself slowly out and gazed across the field to the south, protecting his eyes from the glare off a fresh layer of snow, his jaw fell slack in shock.

Not three-hundred yards away, and closing in on their own lair at a frightening pace, were at least a dozen riders on horseback.

And that could only mean one thing...

BETRAYED

"We are betrayed!" Brother de Berens yelled. "They have come."

"Who has come, Brother?" Nickolas de Thackere demanded. Along with all the others he was suddenly on full alert.

"A dozen riders. The King's Guard. Brothers, we have been undone."

"By whom?" Hassall asked, his voice deep and firm.

"There is no time to concern ourselves with whom, if what Brother Davide says is true."

"It is true, my friend," he confirmed.

"Then we must meet them full on. Brothers, take up your arms."

"We have but moments before they are here," warned Brother de Berens. "We must hurry."

Calm and composed, the elder of their order,

Brother James de Somervila, took up his sword and rallied his men into action. Less than a minute later, all six of the rogue Templars had eased themselves out of the secret cave system and stood in a wide semi-circle. Their feet sunk deep in the snow, and their hot breath formed mist clouds in front of their faces. The air was gelid, the ground beneath the layer of snow frozen solid. But despite the cold, within their strong chests all hearts beat with a heat and strength born of fearless confidence. They were Templars. Warrior Monks. Men who had sworn an oath of allegiance to their Grand Master Bernard when they were accepted into the order, but who had been let down by those tainted by fear; first and foremost, the coward Pope Clement V of Avignon.

The Pope had always feared the growing power and reach of the Templars. Through a series of authoritarian moves and strategically applied pressure on the right Kings of Europe and beyond, he had gradually whittled that power away, until all that remained of the once mighty Order of the Knights Templar were a few rogue bands forced into hiding.

Well, not any more. After today, the Pope knew, the Templars would be resigned to the history books.

"Woah there," yelled the lead rider, pulling back hard on the reins and easing his powerful mount to a stop some fifty yards from the bastard Templars. They had just taken up a semi-circle position on the open ground. It was as if they had materialised from the very snow-covered ground beneath them, for there seemed to be nowhere else to have hidden. Their informant had told him it was a cave system, but he hadn't told him the entrance to it was out in the open. He had expected it to be within some kind of rocky outcrop, where they could use stealth to approach without being seen. It mattered little. The Templars were feared fighters. But six men, even Templars, could do nothing against twelve mounted Knights of the King's Guard.

The rest of the lead rider's men pulled in behind him, though all remained in their saddles. The robed man stayed toward the back. Leaning over to the guard nearest him, he said something, and a message was passed forward. Once it reached the lead man, he nodded. Steeling himself with a deep breath, he jumped down from his stead and stood tall, trying hard to conceal his growing unease. He wasn't afraid of any man, especially with eleven hardened war veterans at his shoulder. He wasn't afraid. But then again, the six men before him did not look afraid either. And they should have been afraid. They should have been fearing not only for their lives, but for their very souls under the wrath of God.

"I am commanded by my master, Kind Edward II, to take you by whatever means necessary to stand trial for heresy. I recommend that you lay down your arms and surrender peacefully."

Standing to James de Somervila's right, Brother Daren de Hassall laughed. It was the laugh of a man without much of a care in the world. Deep yet joyous, it soon had the other Templars beside him chuckling too. They got the joke before he had even said it.

"Now you listen to me, you snivelling scullery maid. I only have one arm, and I am not laying that down for you, nor anyone else for that matter. If you want it, you will have to come and get it."

More chuckles followed, but beneath their smiles the rogue Templars were readying themselves for a fight to the death. They would not be disappointed.

William de Gravelle, leader of the King's Guard, narrowed his eyes. He had expected a swift capture of the rogue men. Based on their reaction to his recommendation of surrendering, however, it was going to be anything but swift. *So be it*, he thought. De Gravelle turned to his men.

"Make it quick. The King wants them alive. But he did not say anything about them being in one piece. Get the bastards."

"Ready boys?" growled James de Somervila. "Let us do thine duty."

Without waiting for any further orders, the rogue Templars, led by the ferocious blades of Brothers de Somervila and Hassall, attacked the dozen King's Guards before they even had time to draw their swords.

De Gravelle was first to fall, his head hitting the ground before his body, blood spraying in great arcs from his severed carotid artery and staining the virgin snow in swathes of dark crimson. Horses reared, and other stunned guards fell from their mounts, unprepared to be attacked after expecting to be the aggressors. Several of them jarred their mounts into charges, swords swinging wildly. Yet the first assault was to no avail.

Arcing around, they returned to find three more of their number already slain, guts spilled in great steaming heaps onto the snow, their horses unharmed and bolting away across the whitewashed fields.

Finding himself suddenly engaged in a two versus one situation, Daren de Hassall was in his element against the road-weary King's Guards. They were decent fighters, but were no match for a thirty-year Crusade veteran. Despite having just one arm, his one arm was better than their four combined. He had chopped them down in mere seconds, their anguished, agonised cries travelling far across the thin air of the valley. They soon fell silent.

In less than five minutes, seven of the King's men were dead. Three more had turned their horses and fled for reinforcements. Three lay prone on the ground, their injuries rendering them useless. Only one man was unaccounted for... it was the man dressed as a peasant.

Young Brother Deane de Tourville scanned the

snowy landscape, his sharp eyes soon catching sight of fluttering brown robes disappearing into a small copse of trees no more than quarter of a mile away.

"Go on, Brother Tourville. Ride him down and bring him back here. I think I know who he is, but to believe it I need to see it with my own eyes."

Deane de Tourville snagged the reins of one of the horses that hadn't bolted and mounted it with one graceful swing of a powerful leg. A moment later he was chasing down the man apparently fleeing for his life. Whoever he was, Deane knew, he probably had only a few minutes to live.

The man had ducked into the copse of trees. They didn't offer much protection, stripped bare of leaves after two months of harsh winter. Deane slid off the horse and draped the reins over the branch of a tree. On foot, he followed the man's fresh tracks through the snow. There was nowhere to hide, except behind one of the thicker tree trunks. Deane prepared himself for the attack he felt sure was imminent.

Yet, he was not concerned. The man was only wearing the tattered robes of a peasant. If he was armed, it was not with anything substantial. It would be an easy chore to apprehend him and take him —

He didn't see him. Didn't even hear him approach. The knife plunged deep into his back, just below the ribs on his left side, and he fell to a knee.

He twisted his neck to look behind him and froze in shock.

"But you are... You are –"

"Dead? No, not dead, Brother Tourville. In fact, I am very much alive. Unlike you will be in a couple of minutes... I am afraid I have administered a mortal wound upon you. I would rather not have had to kill you, but alas, it seems I have no choice. Because I will not die here today. Thus, it is either you or me. And that is an easy –"

Stephen de Stapelbrigg did not finish his sentence. Brother Deane swung his sword up so fast that the older, more sluggish de Stapelbrigg did not react swiftly enough. The blade hacked clean through his elbow, both arm and dagger falling to the snow with a dull thud.

Deane eased himself to his feet, wincing in agony from his own wound but certain it was not as bad as de Stapelbrigg had said. Nevertheless, he did not want the others to know he was injured. He looked down at de Stapelbrigg. He was lying in the snow, whimpering, and trying hard to clutch his remaining hand against the stump of his opposite arm, desperate to stem the stream of blood.

Deane knew he would cause him no further problems. He stripped off his own robe and grabbed handfuls of snow, pushing them hard against his wound, trying to numb the pain. With gritted teeth, the young Templar fought back the growing nausea.

Working quickly, he stripped a length of fabric from de Stapelbrigg's tunic and wrapped it around his lower torso, pulling it tight and knotting the two ends to hold it in place. It was agonising, but the icy snow was beginning to ease that pain. He slipped his tunic back over his shoulders and turned his attention to the treacherous man before him. The others would surely want to question him... he needed to get him back before he perished.

His own injury could wait. Questioning the traitor could not.

He placed a noosed rope around de Stapelbrigg's neck, then mounted the horse. His face etched in pain, the young Knight led the horse and captive out of the trees and back towards the cave complex.

A VOW OF SILENCE

"Ah, there he is. Very good, Brother Deane. Very good."

James de Somervila approached his younger companion and smiled, watching as he slid off the horse and led the apprehended man over to the group.

"Here he is, Brother James. I, uh... well, he laid down an arm." Deane grinned at the joke, but he had only said it to distract the Brothers from his injury.

"Excellent," bellowed Daren de Hassall as he approached, slapping Deane on the shoulder, causing the young Templar to wince in agony. No one saw it. Internally Deane felt like screaming.

Hassall fixed his eyes on the man before him. Then those eyes narrowed. Then they opened again in wild fury, and he stepped forward and slapped de Staplebrigg so hard his head nearly flew right off his shoulders. "Fucking traitor!" he yelled, and slapped him again, the powerful backhander sending him to his knees.

"Why? Why have you turned against your Brothers, de Stapelbrigg?"

Stephen de Stapelbrigg could not answer. He was almost unconscious, and nothing he could say would make any difference to the outcome of this drama anyway. He knew he was a dead man.

Brother James de Somervila stepped between Hassall and de Stapelbrigg. "Enough, Brother Daren," he said quietly, and Hassall obeyed. He stepped away, muttering something about traitorous bastards as he did.

James de Somervila knelt down beside de Stapelbrigg. They had believed the man to be dead. One of their brethren had informed them that their former Brother had been killed when thrown from his horse a month previous. Since he had not returned to the caves, they had assumed it was true. Thus, it was almost like looking at a ghost, not least because the loss of blood had paled his skin so much it now matched the snow around him.

"Why have you betrayed us, Brother? You were one of us. What has changed?"

Stephen de Stapelbrigg looked up at the man knelt before him. His breaths were ragged and he knew he was dying. The truth was, he had made a mistake. He had made many, but none was worse than betraying a fellow Templar. He had not truly believed in the same things these few men had believed in on the Crusades in the Holy Land. He was a pure Christian, a servant of God. Yes, some of it had appealed to him then. Far away from home, on foreign shores, exhausted from travel and delirious from the constant battles... There had been some solace in the bizarre customs and rituals of their... their enemy.

But these men were... different? Yes, different. That was true. But were they still loyal to the same God as him? Yes they were. And yet de Stapelbrigg had given up their location to King Edward's Royal Guards. And for what? Peace? After serving in the Crusades de Stapelbrigg knew he would never find any of that. So, what then? The purse of gold he was to receive on his return to Berkeley Castle? He knew he would never make it back to the castle alive now.

Then what? The answer was so simple he would have smiled if he could. But he could not. Stephen de Stapelbrigg had worn his last smile. He was seconds from drawing his last breath.

"Why, Brother de Stapelbrigg? What has caused you to have betrayed us?"

De Stapelbrigg fought hard to raise his eyes to the eyes of his old friend James. His breaths faltered. A single tear formed in the corner of his right eye, almost freezing where it lay. He sucked in a final, raspy breath, and whispered, "For nothing."

Stephen de Stapelbrigg's eyes closed for the last time. He was dead.

And from that moment forth, he would go down in history as the man who betrayed the last of the Templar Knights.

"What now?" asked Nickolas de Thackere. "Our location here is known. The King's men will be back in days. Where will we go?"

Brother de Berens answered. "South. We go south. I know just the place. We will leave a coded message behind us, for any true Brother who might happen upon it. And we go south."

"And what about these three bastards?" asked de Thackere. "Shall we let them go?"

"No!" James de Somervila's short answer left no one in any doubt as to its meaning. "No. We cannot let them go. We need to make an example of them." He glanced at Daren de Hassall, who nodded. A moment later, all three men were dead, slaughtered where they lay, their blood tainting the snow. Next their heads were removed, and Brothers de Thackere and de Berens were charged with stowing them in plain sight in the barren trees, where any passing King's Guards would find them. The message was clear; Leave us alone, or die.

James de Somervila turned to congratulate his protégé, Brother Deane, on capturing Stapelbrigg so easily. He could not immediately spot him. When he did, his heart skipped several beats. Laying in the snow behind the horse, the youngest of their rogue band of Templars was unmoving, a large swathe of crimson staining the ground around him. De Somervila raced to his side and flipped him over, searching for the source of the blood, soon finding the horrific blade wound beneath his tunic. In an instant he knew it was too late.

He grabbed Deane's face between his strong hands, forcing the young Templar to look at him. "You have been my greatest triumph, young Deane," he whispered, "and you have honoured the code of the Templars. Your death will not be in vain. You have helped us keep our secret. A secret that must remain forever and always thus. Farewell, my Brother. You are the very best of us."

Brother Deane de Tourville's eyelids fluttered once, then twice, then fell still. His eyes remained open, but unseeing. The youngest of James de Somervila's rogue band of Templar Knights was gone, slain by a treacherous coward.

When all the remaining Brothers returned, their number reduced to five after the death of de Tourville, James de Somervila called them together.

"My Brothers... my friends... we know we must leave this place now. The King's Guards will surely return. But this is no longer simply about our own self-preservation. What we learned on the Crusades in the Holy Land... what we *know*... must remain known only to us, until such time that others are ready to learn and accept all that we know. It is our duty to our fellow man to keep this knowledge secret, and we must succeed, for our countrymen are not ready for the consequences of our failure. Do you all agree?"

After a moment's silence, in which each of the rogue Templars took a few seconds to comprehend the new vow they were being asked to take, they nodded. None of them gathered there on that snow-covered ground in Shropshire had ever swayed from their original vows, sworn to their Grand Master in a solemn ceremony when they were accepted into the Holy order. None of them, not even the younger Brother de Tourville, had erred once. And nor would they err from this new vow now.

All five men said a silent prayer, asking for the strength to do what they knew was right... what they knew they must.

In all things to do with what they had learned on the Crusades in the Holy Land, it was a vow of silence.

686 years later

YE OLDE TRIP TO JERUSALEM

Friday 22nd December, 1994

Nottingham

For Hiram Kane, the rest of the university year had passed in a blur of research, writing and procrastinating in the pub, and before he knew it, the Christmas holidays were upon him again. He was looking forward to a relaxing month away from the books... and spending more time with Alex.

Hiram and Alexandria Ridley had become more or less inseparable over the last couple of months. Along with Evan Craft, one of Hiram's closest childhood friends, the three had become a tight-knit group. And, of course, regular drinking partners. Hiram and Alex, however, had learned they shared more than just a love of beer and the Korean martial art of tae-kwon-do. Although they weren't officially a couple, most people who knew them or saw them together suspected it was only a matter of time.

Alexandria Ridley was a British citizen of mixed heritage. Her English father was a professor of literature and her mother was a museum curator from the Egyptian city of Alexandria. It was where she was born, hence the couple naming their only child Alexandria. Yet, she had only lived there until just before her first birthday, when the family relocated back to the UK for her father's new job.

Sadly, when she was just sixteen, Alex's parents were both killed in a car accident, leaving her an orphan. Over the next few years life had dealt her some tough hands, and at times the adversity — as well as her own weaknesses — had almost gotten the better of her. But she had struggled through, and after seeing the light on a backpacking trip in southeast Asia, Alex had emerged from the darkness an impressive, not to mention ambitious, young woman.

Now she was enrolled at the University of East Anglia in Norwich, studying art history at the School of World Art Studies and Museology. It was the same school as Hiram, though lately his studies focused more on archaeology. Hiram was in the final year of his Master's degree, while Alex was still in the second year of her graduate degree. Hiram was a year older than Alex. For different reasons Alex's entry into further education had been set back a years. Hiram didn't know the reasons, and the timing had never seemed right to ask why. He sensed Alex had a few skeletons in her closet, and for now she was keeping the closet door firmly closed.

It was the first weekend of the winter break. The three friends – they rarely did anything separately these days – promised another friend from uni, Luke, that they'd visit him in his native Nottingham for pre-Christmas drinks. On the Friday afternoon they drove up in Hiram's clapped out old Mini Clubman Estate – so old, in fact, it was the model that still had the wooden swing doors on the back – and arrived in the city just after four... and just as the first snowfall of the year coated the ground. Luke told them he'd meet them at his favourite pub, the evocatively named *Ye Olde Trip to Jerusalem*, and by the time they'd arrived, huddled deep into their insufficient coats, Luke was several beers into his Christmas holiday.

SAINT NICK

"I wouldn't if I were you."

Hiram turned from his position at the bar to see one of the largest — and possibly one of the oldest — men he'd ever laid eyes on. The man sat perched upon not one but two bar stools, his considerable frame sprawled on the far end of the bar. The man had huge, rounded shoulders, and a massive head sat atop an impossibly thick neck. What little hair he had was pure white, and his long, straggly beard was only a few shades darker. Hiram tried hard to ignore the obvious seasonal comparisons with Santa Claus. But Evan couldn't help himself.

From his seat at a table next to the bar, he said, "Shouldn't you be getting ready for, you know, Christmas or something?"

The old man didn't flinch, not even a flicker of a

smile. Instead, his eyes narrowed, fixing on Evan's. He remained silent.

"Uh, sorry," Evan said. "I meant no offence."

The old man turned and resumed his position leaning on the wooden bar, his head shaking slightly in disdain as he slugged down a pint of real ale in three swift gulps. The tankard looked like a shot glass in his gigantic hand.

"What?" Evan asked, smirking as Hiram, Alex and Luke stared at him.

"Really?" Hiram said quietly. "Santa Claus? How the hell old are you?" he added, but couldn't keep the smile from his eyes.

"Don't tell me you weren't thinking the same thing," Evan continued. None of them denied it. The man really did look like the common representation of St. Nick... minus the jovial smile.

"Anyway," Alex said, "what did he mean when he said 'I wouldn't if I were you?'"

"Ah, silly old bugger's probably talking about that old galleon up there," Luke answered. "The one Hiram was about to touch."

"What about it?" Hiram asked, placing down their freshly-poured pints of Holy Grail ale, appropriate for a pub named Ye Olde Trip to Jerusalem. "Is it cursed or something?"

"Funnily enough," Luke said, "it is. At least, that's the legend. As I told you earlier, this pub's ancient, twelfth century I think. Probably like the old timer," he whispered, eliciting a round of admittedly childish chuckling. Luke continued. "Apparently the crusaders used to meet here and drink before heading off to the Holy Land, er, crusading? There're loads of stories of ghosts and legends surrounding this old boozer... one of the most famous is about that galleon." Luke cast his eyes to the mini wood-carved galleon sat above the bar. The others followed with their eyes.

The galleon was small, about a yard long, its mast a yard tall. It looked as ancient as the pub itself. It was almost completely blackened with age, likely from the wood fires that kept the pub warm in winter, just as they were now. The pub itself lies directly beneath the mound with Nottingham Castle perched on top. Some of the pub's rooms are literally carved out of the very rock itself; they're essentially underground caves. All these elements only added to the unique surroundings.

Luke continued. "Legend has it that —"

"— that anyone who's ever come into contact with that old relic has met with a sudden, mysterious and gruesome death?" The huge old man's strong voice cut Luke off. He hadn't turned and still faced the bar. When he at last spun to face them, his eyes wide and dark, each of the four friends sat at the table believed he was looking directly at them. The difference between popular images of Saint Nicholas — seen everywhere at this time of year — and the man at the bar, was that St. Nick is portrayed as a pleasantly plump rotund old man. There was nothing rotund about this chap. He was, quite simply, a solid stack of beef, albeit well-aged. His deep voice rumbled on.

"The galleon is cursed, and I can tell you for certain that those are not just haunted pub myths, no sir." The huge man's barrel chest rose and fell for a few seconds, then he seemed to regain some composure. He spoke again, this time in a quieter voice. "But that is by no means the best story I could tell you. No sir..." He paused, gauging their reaction. Glancing around, and satisfied, he asked, "May I join you?"

The pub's upper room was quiet, and the girl behind the bar had suddenly made herself scarce. Alex got the sense she had already heard the story about to be told several times too many.

"Sure thing," Evan said. "Please, grab a seat. Sorry about before."

"It's okay, son," the man said. "I'm used to it." He smiled, and it was genuine. "I had to say something when I saw you reaching up to touch the galleon," he said, tipping his head in Hiram's direction. "I know most people wouldn't believe in the curse, but... But, let's just say I know how dangerous it is."

"Did something... has someone you know been... cursed?" Alex asked. She, like the others, didn't believe in such superstitious nonsense. Yet the man's sincere and solemn manner had snagged their attention.

"Yes." His answer was sure and sudden, as if he meant it with his entire being.

"Could you tell us a little about the legend?" Luke asked. "I mean, I've heard a few crappy stories, but nothing too serious."

The old man leant back in his chair and took a long drink of his new pint. Then he finished the rest off in one more swig and called out to the girl pretending to be busy behind the bar. "Five more pints of ale please, lassie," he said. At last he smiled. "Sure, I could tell you about the curse of that old galleon up there. I could. But I'm not going to."

The friends shared curious glances, disappointed, and almost annoyed by the huge man's cryptic words. The disappointment didn't last long.

"I have a much better story than that. Are you kids ready to be amazed?"

A FEW FLAWED MEN

"Like most things, it all started with a few flawed men."

Alex scoffed. "Like everything, you mean?" she said, casting her intense green eyes first at Hiram, then at Evan. She glared, but there was mischief behind the stare.

The big man chuckled, and it was the laugh of a man who believed he'd found a like-minded tribe. "But before I tell you the story, I'll mention another flawed man. Me. My name's Steven... Steven Stalbridge. What I'm about to tell you I've only ever told to a few people befo —"

There came an audible scoff from an unseen source somewhere behind the bar, and Alex knew her hunch about the girl was right.

Unperturbed, Steven continued. "Apparently I've... well, I was once told that I'm a descendent of a famous Templar Knight, and that I'm the last in a long line of —"

"You're descended from the Templars? For real?" Hiram's eyes were wide with awe. "I loved reading about the Knights Templar when I was a kid... reckon I've read every book there is on the Templars. A real Templar descendent?"

"Yes... apparently."

"Who was the knight you're descended from?" Luke asked, equally as amazed as Hiram. Luke had been in this so-called Crusader pub dozens of times and had heard the stories and legends about the escapades of the Knights Templar. But he'd never met anyone claiming to have the blood of a Templar Knight coursing through his or her veins. Steven had asked them if they were ready to be amazed. Hiram and Luke were more than ready.

"His name was something de Drayton, or *'of Drayton'*, wherever that is, and it's believed he was the last known living Templar in the United Kingdom. I think I overheard... " Steven nodded in Luke's direction, eyebrows raised.

"Luke."

"I think I overheard young Luke there telling you about the history of this pub. About it being the last staging post of many Crusaders before they went off to the Holy Land?"

"Yes, he did," Alex said. "Fascinating stuff."

"Well," Steven said, his voice low, "there's a lot of

Templar history in England that you won't find in any books. You might want to get another round of drinks... it's quite the tale."

Hiram stood and skirted through the chairs to the bar. He was soon joined by Evan, while Alex and Luke stayed with Steven.

"What do you make of the old timer?" Evan asked. "I mean, he's quirky isn't he."

"Seems legit enough to me, if not a little mysterious." Hiram glanced up at the musty wooden galleon above his head, tempted to reach up and touch. Instead, he glanced over at Steven, whose narrowed eyes were fixed so pointedly on his in that he almost recoiled. Very subtly, Steven shook his head, but it left Hiram in no doubt that he was not to touch the galleon. Not at any cost.

It only added to the old man's mystique. Hiram Kane didn't believe in ancient curses or any other such nonsense, though he did love studying them at university under the tutelage of world-renowned professor John O'nians. Hiram did believe in respecting his elders, however. He left the galleon alone.]

Hiram and Evan to the table laden with several pints and an appetite for a good story.

"Cheers, to one and all," Steven said, his voice now loud and enthusiastic.

To Hiram it almost seemed as if he'd been waiting years to tell his story and, finally, had a suitable — perhaps worthy — audience. Based on his decidedly ancient appearance, not to mention having the physique of a Templar Knight, Hiram mused that the old man might well have been waiting since the twelfth-century.

DISC OF GOLD

The Kane Estate, Norfolk / Suffolk Border, England
Summer, 1988

"I have a surprise for you."

Hiram knew that when their grandfather gave his grandkids surprises, they were always unique, always special, and had been chosen with a specific reason or purpose in mind. Thus, as his grandfather said the words to Hiram now his eyes widened with excitement. Not for long, however.

"Close your eyes, my boy," said his grandfather. Hiram did as instructed. A moment later a small package was placed gently into his open palms.

"Now open your eyes again, son. Go ahead, open it."

With great care belying his young hands, Hiram

eagerly pulled open the folded brown wrapping paper and spread it out on his lap. He gasped, his mouth forming a generous O as he took in what he saw. Threaded over a long, brown leather necklace was a dazzling disk of gold. It was two inches across, and this, perhaps a quarter inch thick. It felt surprisingly heavy in his hands. In the dusky, late afternoon East Anglian sun the burnished disc glowed, almost ethereal. Ten-year-old Hiram was immediately enamoured by the magical object.

"Well, put it on then," encouraged his grandfather, delight clear in the creases of his eyes.

Hiram lifted the leather cord over his head and eased it down over his neck. The shimmering talisman came to rest in the centre of his chest. It was a beautiful object. Though Hiram doubted it had much intrinsic value, to him it was totally priceless. It instantly became his pride and joy.

"My own father gave it to me a few years before he died," said Hiram's granddad, known in the family as *Hiram Snr*. "Now I want you to have it. Your great-grandfather Patrick found it on that expedition with Bingham in the Sacred Valley in Peru way back in nineteen-eleven. Do you know what it is?"

"Um, yes... I think it's Incan?" Hiram's grandfather nodded. "Is it a sun disc? An object to honour the Sun God... Inti?"

"Exactly, my boy. Exactly." The old-timer beamed, proud of his grandson's knowledge. "And that's exactly the reason you should have it... because you care. About history. About culture. So, now it's yours."

Hiram pulled his eyes away from the mesmerising artefact. "Is it real? I mean, is it really Inca gold, Granddad?"

"Yes, my boy, it most certainly is. Real Inca gold... Atahualpa's gold."

Hiram's fingers once more lifted the dazzling disk of gold away from his chest, his eyes fixed upon it. Without warning, his mind's eyes suddenly set off wandering to faraway lands, as thoughts of lost cities and mountain exploration and jungles and adventures flitted through his mind.

His grandfather Hiram Snr recognised the expression on his grandson's face. That look of awe, the expression of wonder. And he recognised it because it had been inherited directly from him.

THE STONE MAN

Back in the pub, the conversation continued.

"You're from Nottingham, Luke?" Steven confirmed. Luke nodded. "So I'll ask you a question. Have you ever heard of The Stone Man?"

Luke's brow furrowed as a hint of recognition flitted for a moment. Whether it were from having had too many beers or genuinely not remembering, nothing about a stone man came to mind. "No, I don't think so. Why, what is it?"

"Well, how about St. Giles? Do you know Saint Giles Church?"

"Yes, I do. I have to walk past it whenever I come into town."

"Okay, good," Steven replied. "Standing beside the entrance to the main part of the church is somewhat of an odd statue. It's a stone-carved figure of a man, but it's in terrible condition and most locals have no idea who it's supposed to be or where it came from."

"But you know who it is?" Hiram asked. It wasn't really a question.

Steven's eyes were alive with mischief. "It just so happens that yes, I do. Well, not exactly who... What."

"What do you mean, what?" Luke asked.

"I mean, I don't know his name, but I know what he is?"

"Then what is he?" Evan probed.

"Yes," said Alex, her curiosity piqued, "what is he?"

Hiram didn't ask. Somehow, he knew.

Steven said, "A Templar Knight."

Okay, now we're getting somewhere, Hiram mused.

"You said nobody knows where he came from," Luke said. "Does that mean he wasn't always at the church?"

"Exactly. There're ancient photos that prove the Stone Man was once situated in a field a few miles outside town. He was positioned at the fork of what were once several old country lanes leading into ancient Nottingham, but are now main roads. Legend suggests that his position wasn't at all random, and in fact..."

"In fact what?" Hiram asked, sensing something exciting was coming.

"... that the Stone Man was in fact a marker. Perhaps a sign post, pointing the way to a secret Templar location... somewhere out west of here."

"You mean like some kind of a map?" Alex suggested.

"Exactly, young lady. A map. Of course, one stone statue couldn't lead directly to wherever the secret place was. But as part of a bigger set up? Why not?"

"And I suppose you know where it leads to?" Evan's cynical nature meant he doubted almost everything anyone ever told him. Including this.

"All I know is what the legend says." Steven's eyes shone with adventure.

"Which is?" Evan said through a doubtful smirk.

"Apparently there's a secret cave system somewhere in what is now Shropshire,. Those caves were used by the last known Templar Knights in this country to hide from the King's Guards, who were hunting them down like rabbits. The guards had been ordered to round up all Templars under the charge of heresy and blasphemy. You've all heard of Friday the thirteenth, of course?"

"Yes, great movie," Evan said, "though I preferred A Nightmare on Elm Street." He shook his head, sarcasm dripping from every word.

"Isn't Friday the thirteenth related to Halloween?" Luke asked.

"Yes and no," Hiram answered. Steven grinned

as Hiram continued. "These days it's synonymous with Halloween, correct. But if I'm not mistaken, Friday the thirteenth, in the year 1307, is when King Philip the Fourth of France had hundreds, maybe thousands of Templar Knights murdered in their sleep for being heretics. That was the official line. In truth, he just wanted their fortune and lands." Hiram glanced at Steven for some acknowledgment he was right. It came in an instant.

"That's exactly right, young fellow," the old man said. "And you know who was among those rounded up in England?"

"Your ancestor," Hiram said. "The Templar Knight you're descend from."

"Right again. Meaning, if the rumours are true, then I'm a direct descendent of one of the last heroic Templars of England, falsely accused of heresy, hunted down, and slain like a common criminal. I know the truth about what happened is out there, but..." Steven paused, more than a hint of sadness in his eyes. "Well, I'm an old man now, too old to go gallivanting around the country any more. However..." He paused again, once more gauging their reaction. Steven's eyes crinkled, and his huge head nodded almost imperceptibly, as if to himself. "However, I wonder if you guys might want to go on what might be called a kind of quest for the Holy Grail? My Holy Grail... the truth."

"What?" Evan almost choked on his beer. "A grail quest? Are you kidding?"

Steven's smile faded. He wasn't kidding. Not kidding at all. "Yes, a grail quest. But don't be confused. Not all grail quests seek treasure, or silly golden cups... For me, the grail would simply be the truth about what happened to my ancestor. I believe he was killed somewhere in Shropshire, and that the Stone Man is the first — and nearest — of a series of clues that will ultimately lead to that truth. To my truth. My grail. So, I ask you... do you accept?"

Hiram Kane's eyes were wide with the thrill of Steven's story. Alex looked at him. She recognised that look in his eyes, and she smiled. She loved that about Hiram, loved that he was adventurous like her. Luke was all smiles too, though that was in large part to the half-dozen pints of Holy Grail ale they'd consumed. Only Evan had yet to smile. In his mind it was just another story by just another delusional old man in a pub. He'd heard a few over the years, but he had to admit Steven's story was better than most.

Hiram looked at his friends, then at the old man. "Mister Stalbridge, I —"

"Call me Steven, please."

"Okay, Steven. Steven, I accept. And if my friends don't want to join me, I shall go alone. I'll find the truth for you. I'll find your grail."

"I'll go too," Luke said.

"You're not going without me," confirmed Alex.

All eyes turned to Evan Craft now. He sat still, lips to his pint, feeling judged as his eyes stared back at each of them over the pint tankard, challenging them to convince him it wasn't all just some bullshit story from some lonely old man seeking a little attention during his nightly quest to get hammered.

"So, Evan..." Hiram said. "You know I have a little money, right? I propose a road trip. What about if I buy the rest of the food and beers on this spontaneous road trip? Meaning... if you don't come with us... you'll miss out."

Evan's eyes locked on his oldest friend's. Hiram's family had a deserved reputation around the world for being great adventurers. Hiram's great-grandfather Patrick had been Hiram Bingham's assistant when the American scholar rediscovered the lost Incan city of Machu Picchu. His grandfather, Hiram Snr, was also responsible for many great archaeological discoveries, and now held an important position at the world famous British Museum. With that fame came a certain amount of wealth, and although not one single part of the younger Hiram's brain worked materialistically, he did enjoy using his money for treating his friends.

Evan fought hard to suppress the grin forming behind his pint, but his eyes betrayed him. Besides, he was a sucker for a free lunch.

"Fine," he said, "I'll humour you on your wild

goose chase quest for this holy grail. But only if you're buying tonight's beers too."

Hiram rolled his eyes, then grinned. "Done deal." He turned to Steven. "So how about that legend?" he asked. "What do you think happened to those last slain Templars?"

"Slain?" He grinned, mischief in his eyes. "Well," Steven said, now in his element, "despite the common belief among scholars that the last of the Templars in England, including my ancestor, were hunted down and killed, even after they had been absolved by the Pope, legend suggests that some of them escaped. Now, you don't need me to tell you that the Templars had to swear oaths of poverty. But despite that, many of them had managed to amass great wealth over the years of their service. Along with that wealth came power, which was ultimately to be their undoing. Jealousy is a powerful human trait, and like I said, the will of a few flawed men let the fear of that wealth and power get the better of them. Ultimately, it brought about the demise of the Templars."

"But you don't believe it?" asked Hiram.

"I believe the Templars as an official organisation is finished, yes. But do I think some of them survived? Do I believe that a few rogue bands of those men didn't succumb to the will of the Pope and outlived him, living out their lives in secret, and leaving behind a legacy that still exists today? Well, yes I do. I believe that with my whole heart."

"And if we find evidence of that, find the truth about what happened to them, and what happened to your ancestor, we will have found your Holy Grail?"

Steven Stalbridge fell silent for long moments, his huge shoulders rising and falling gently as emotion threatened to bring a tear to his eye. He was eighty-three years old, though his appearance belied his physicality. He was still more than capable of the odd adventure. The truth was, Steven was scared. He was scared of finding the truth, afraid it might not be what he wanted to hear. A decade ago he had decided to stop chasing that truth, stop seeking that which might ruin everything he'd believed in all his long years. That is, until Hiram Kane came into his pub.

Finally, he spoke, the threat of tears passed. "That is what I believe. Yes. You will find proof that I am who I have long believed myself to be. Then this old man will die happy in the knowledge he was a descendent of a heroic Templar Knight."

"Well in that case," Hiram said, "we'll set off first thing in the morning. And we'll start at the Stone Man."

TOMMY

Despite nursing mild hangovers, the friends were up early and relishing the sense of an imminent adventure.

Hiram Kane, Alex Ridley, Evan Craft and Luke Richardson had congregated in the cosy kitchen of Luke's rented terrace house. He had made them all bacon sandwiches, and with several cups of tea to wash them down, they were too ready for the day. Next they squeezed into Hiram's Mini Clubman, and by nine-thirty they were making the short drive from Luke's house to Saint Giles Church, just on the outskirts of Nottingham.

Whether it was because of the late night in the pub, or the gentle hangovers, or the cold — they'd awoken to a frosty, snowy morning, the pale, wintry light almost ethereal — there was little chatter among the friends, who usually bantered non stop. For

Hiram's part it was none of the above. It was more a sense of the adventure he felt, the very idea of a kind of grail quest simply mesmerising to the young archaeology graduate. Of course, he knew it was unlikely it would turn out to be anything of the sort. But that didn't dampen his appetite for it... not even close.

Luke was simply intrigued by it all, and felt in a kind of wonder. Of course he had many friends in his native city of Nottingham, but none were like his university friends. These guys were different, interested in the same things he was. He'd found in them like-minded people he could trust and be himself around, something he relished.

Evan was usually the most effervescent of the group. Usually. He had never been a morning person, so the last thing he wanted was to turn out on a freezing cold morning in a city he didn't know on some ridiculous grail quest, all because of the lame story of some crazy old man. Hiram was right... he would do anything for a free lunch. But this, just days before Christmas? Bah humbug didn't even do justice to how little he was enjoying himself. He hunkered down a little further in his coat, hoping to grab some extra sleep and be awoken only when they all realised it was a complete waste of everyone's time.

Alex sat quietly, gazing out of the steamed up window. Like Hiram, she was excited. But that excitement was tempered. Alex had an uneasy feeling that not everything was as they thought. She didn't honestly believe there would be any danger. It was more a sense of negativity, perhaps even bad news. She had no idea of course. For now she'd sit back and enjoy the ride. Besides, she was riding alongside her handsome, interesting and relatively new love interest, Hiram Kane. And that was just fine by her.

It wasn't long before Hiram eased his crowded Mini to a stop in the snowy car park next to Saint Giles church. They all clambered out, Evan grumbling something incoherent as he pulled his woolly hat a little further down over his ears.

"Right, shall we check out this stone man?" Hiram asked, leading his friends towards the main entrance of the church. There weren't many people about. Christmas was just a couple of days away, and Hiram figured most people were out and about, busy wasting money on useless gifts that would likely be in landfill come the new year. *Consumerism, just one more curse of the modern day,* he mused as they approached the apparently deserted church.

The snow fell heavier now, so they hustled through the sturdy wooden doors into the sanctuary of the church. There was no sign of a stone man where they had expected to find it.

"Good morning," came a voice from an unseen source, startling them in the empty church. They turned to see a vicar approaching. His eyes betrayed his curiosity at the guests to his church he'd never seen before. "May I assume you are *not* here for this morning's carol service?" he asked, a trace of good humour in his voice.

"Good morning, Father," Alex replied. "You're right, we're not here for the carols, though I'm sure it would be lovely."

"Then what brings you to my humble church on this beautiful day? It's certainly not for the warmth," the vicar said, visibly shivering in the chill of the large empty space. "I'm sure it's colder in here than it is out there." The man's smile was warmer than they all felt.

"Actually," Luke said, "maybe you can help us?"

"It's my job to help those in need," he said, a sparkle in his eyes. "So, how can I help?"

"Father, we're —"

"My name's Ian," the vicar said.

"Hello Ian. We're here to find, um, the stone man? We thought it was supposed to be by the entrance, but we didn't see anything there."

"Our Stone Man used to be right outside those doors, as you suggested. I'm afraid to tell you that last winter the cold weather and old age finally caught up with our friend. The stone crumbled, and the poor thing collapsed in a heap of rubble. A sad day indeed."

"Why sad?" Evan asked. "What's so special

about an old stone statue that nobody knows anything about?"

"Who said nobody knows anything about it?" Ian replied, the hint of a grin curling his lip.

"So you do know something?"

Ian thought about his answer for a moment, a pensive expression creasing his brow. He appraised the group of youngsters before him, wondering what, if anything, he should tell them. He figured, however, that since they were already looking for the Stone Man, they must already know what it was and what it meant. Confirming that hunch now now probably wouldn't do any harm.

"I suppose the answer to that question is a simple yes, I do know something. The Stone Man wasn't just a statue. It was an ancient marker, a sign post if you will."

"A sign post to what?" Hiram asked, a surge of hope swelling.

"Legend has it that Tommy was pointing the way to the last known location of the Templar Knights in England."

Hiram nodded, a smile spreading across his face. Ian's story had backed up exactly what Steven Stalbridge had told them in the pub last night. This was shaping up to be something none of them probably imagined, and to Hiram that was very exciting. He felt alive, felt that surge of adrenalin his great-grandfather must've when felt on the cusp of finding

Machu Picchu, and how his grandfather felt when making important archaeological discoveries of his own. Maybe they themselves were on the cusp of some important discovery. There was only one way to find out.

"So do you know where exactly – uh, Tommy? – was pointing to?" he asked. "Or is that still a mystery?"

Ian the vicar smiled now, confident these youngsters were on the right side of the law and harbouring only good intentions. "Hmm, well, there is no official *last* known place of The Templars in this country. But..."

"But what?" Evan asked. "You know?"

"I do have a theory, yes."

"Will you share your theory with us, Ian?" Alex asked. Ian nodded.

"Do you all promise to be careful?"

"Yes, we promise," said Hiram, and Ian believed him.

"Very well. Remember, it's just a theory. In my younger years I was a keen historian. My research told me that there's a cave system somewhere to the west that might... just might... have been the last known location of the Templar Knights in England. Old photographs suggest that when Tommy was originally situated in the countryside ten miles outside of town, the direction in which his arm pointed was directly to that alleged location. It's my belief that the last location of the Templars in England was a little known cave system in a hamlet called Caynton, in the county of Shropshire."

Hiram shared an excited look with his friends. Steven Stalbridge had mentioned Shropshire in the pub last night, and that too had been backed up by Ian. It seemed as if they were definitely onto something.

"Thanks so much for your help, Ian," Hiram said. "We really appreciate it."

"My pleasure. I hope you find what you're searching for."

"Before we go, I have one more question." It was Evan, and he wore a mischievous grin.

"Try me."

"The statue. Why do you call it Tommy?"

Ian smiled, though he seemed a little embarrassed. "Isn't it obvious?" He had always though it was.

"I guess not," replied Evan.

"Tommy. Tommy the Templar."

CAYNTON CAVES

Now they had a firm location to head for, the four friends hustled out of the church and scrambled back into Hiram's Mini. It was now covered in a thick layer of snow.

"Shove the heating on can you?" Evan said. "It's freezing in here."

Hiram turned the heating up full blast as he waited for the windscreen to clear, while the others swept the rest of the car clear of the snow. A couple of minutes later, and with the car sufficiently heated and the windows cleared, they set off. Hiram drove slowly along the snow-covered roads. Fortunately the roads were almost completely devoid of traffic; most people had sensibly opted to walk wherever it was they needed to go in this crappy weather.

Hiram and his friends needed to go west. According to Father Ian back at Saint Giles church, it was approximately seventy miles to the cave complex in Shropshire. Seventy miles wasn't far. But in this weather? The ninety-minute drive might take double that. Luckily the A38 dual carriageway had already been cleared of snow, and after leaving the A38 and joining first the M6 and then the M38 Motorways, they made the journey in a little less than two hours.

The snow storm had finished and the sky was clear and blue by the time they'd arrived just after one o'clock in the afternoon. The clear sky though meant the temperature had dropped further. It was just something else for Evan to whinge about.

But where had they arrived to, exactly? The cave system was allegedly secret, so they didn't expect it to be broadcast anywhere. Ian had told them it definitely wasn't on any tourist maps. Ian had also told them the entrance was apparently slap bang in the middle of a five-sided field south east of the small town of Shifnel. So, after driving around the area a little, mercifully on snow-free roads, they soon found what they believed to be the field Ian mentioned. They left the car and stood at the overgrown gate to the field, next to a sign that boldly informed them it was PRIVATE PROPERTY. From that vantage point there was no obvious entrance to any caves. They would simply have to take a closer look.

"I guess there's nothing for it," Alex said, ignoring the sign and clambering over the gate. Huddling deeper into her jacket, she said, "We'll just have to spread out and survey the field... maybe we'll find something if we get closer."

"Agreed," said Hiram, grinning at her dismissal of the sign but nonetheless casting his gaze about for any sign of a grumpy farmer with a shotgun.

"Let's go," Evan said, apparently more excited by the prospect than he was earlier and clambering over the rusting iron gate, his short legs making it more difficult than it should have been.

The rest of them followed Alex over the gate, that looked as if it had been rusted closed for decades. Upon Hiram's directions, the archaeologist in him taking over, they spread out, walking a few yards apart across the small field — about half as big as a football pitch — in a linear formation. They took the western edge first, and after a few minutes, they reached the far end and turned around. Then they headed back in the opposite direction, but a little farther along. After ten minutes they had covered half the field in an accurate grid pattern. They hadn't found anything.

They turned again and headed back north, and had walked just twenty yards, when Luke yelled out. "Here... I think I've found something."

The others rushed over. At Luke's feet, protruding from the thick layer of snow, was a short wooden stake, barely visible above the snow and weeds. "It's not much, but it couldn't just be random," Luke said. "Could it?"

Not one of them thought it was. Evan was first to react. He stooped down and began scraping away the snow from around the stake. Seconds later he'd revealed a wooden board covered with a layer of muck and weeds. "Someone grab the other side," he said, and Hiram did. They eased it aside with ease, almost certain they'd find some kind of hole beneath it. They weren't disappointed.

There was indeed a hole in the earth, no more than two feet across. Its edges were lined with stone. It would be a tight squeeze, but they'd come all this way... there was simply no way Hiram wasn't going to scramble inside and check it out.

"I think it's safe," he said, "but maybe a couple of us should stay up here, you know, just in case. Any volunteers to stay topside?"

"Me," said Luke. "I... Well, I'm not good in small spaces. It's my height. Guess you could say I'm a also little claustrophobic. If it's alright with you lot I'll happily stay above ground."

"Me too," said Alex. "I'll stay and keep Luke company."

"Great, then me and Ev will check it out. Right Ev?"

"Right," Evan answered. "Someone's got to look after you. Besides, it's freezing out here... might be warmer down there."

Hiram dropped to his knees and leaned down into the hole, shining the torch he'd brought from the car as far as he could reach inside. All he saw was dirt and stone. He realised he'd have to scramble inside just to see where it went. So he did. It took some effort... Hiram was a big man with broad shoulders... but after a few seconds of wriggling he'd disappeared through the hole and out of view. Evan scurried down behind him.

A minute later, both men were out of sight and a butterfly had taken up residence in Alex's gut. She wasn't really afraid – Hiram and Evan could more than look after themselves. But you just never knew. She cast a nervous glance over her shoulder towards where they'd parked the car. A sudden sense of them being watched came to her unbidden. Alex had always believed she was an intuitive person. Not a sixth sense exactly, more like a gut instinct. She trusted those instincts, and they were usually right. But there were no other cars anywhere to be seen, and there was no hint of anyone around the remote field. She put it down to an over-active imagination... perhaps because she cared so much for Hiram.

"Do you think they'll find anything?" Luke asked. "I mean, what the hell could be down there? Surely nothing important, right?"

"I honestly don't know. I mean, Ian said these caves were secret. Steven told us the same thing back at the pub. If there was anything important down there I'm sure someone else would've found it a long time ago."

"That's what I think. I can't imagine there's anything like treasure down there. Maybe another sign though? I mean, like some kind of directions?"

"Hmm, yeah maybe," agreed Alex. "I just hope they aren't gone too long."

HOLY GOATS

Hiram scrambled further along the natural fissure between the rocky walls. It wasn't exactly a cave, more of a narrow tunnel. There wasn't room to even kneel upright, let alone stand, and they dropped to their knees. It was a struggle to move along it. A good place to hide, Hiram had to admit. "You with me?" he said into the darkness behind him, then flashed his torch over his shoulder. Just a few feet back was Evan, easing along like some overgrown beetle.

"Yep, right here. What the hell is this place?"

"I don't know, but it seems as if no one's been here for a while. Shall we keep going?"

"Can't see why not," Evan said. "Go for it."

They scrambled along a little further, perhaps ten yards. Then the tunnel suddenly angled downwards, just as the rocky ceiling rose. Another couple of yards, and Hiram was finally able to stand up, though not to his full height. Evan could stand, and normally Hiram would have teased his oldest mate about his height, or lack thereof. But he didn't. He had spotted something on the floor. A discarded beer can. Several of them in fact. They were crumpled cans of Carlsberg Special Brew... extra strong lager. Whoever had been down here certainly chose their beers with getting drunk in mind. The cans didn't appear that old, and Hiram realised the caves couldn't have been that secret after all.

"Probably just kids from the village," he said.

"No doubt. Great place to bring your first date," Evan agreed. "Shall we push on?"

They edged along the tunnel for another minute, negotiating the gentle left and right turns, and cautious of stumbling as the ground sloped down a little away from them. Another minute, and they came to what seemed to be a dead end. Shining the torch around the cave walls and ceiling, it soon became clear that there had been people this far in before too. Oily stains marred the rock ceiling, as if there had at one time been oil lamps burned here, or at the very least candles.

"Wait, what's that?" Evan's voice came so suddenly it startled Hiram.

"What's what?" he asked. He'd seen nothing other than the old beer cans and oil stains on the stone.

"Give me the torch."

Hiram handed it to Evan, who crouched down and shone it at something low down on the wall. He pointed just above the stony ground. "What is that?"

"Is that a... a carving in the stone?"

"Yeah, looks like it. Back up, give me some room." Hiram backed away a little and Evan stooped down onto his knees again, lowering his head almost to the floor. He fell silent for a moment, studying the scrawled text. It seemed ancient, and appeared to have worn away a fair bit over what he assumed was decades, maybe even hundreds of years. He leaned back and shone the torch at Hiram.

Evan spelled out the word, letter by letter. "P. R. Ō. D. I. T. Ō. R. Prōditōr? Hmm... Now," he said, "I'm no expert, but I'm pretty sure that's Latin. In my opinion, which as you know is always humble, I do believe it says *traitor*."

"Wow, really? You sure?"

"No, not sure at all," Evan conceded. "At best an educated guess."

"Maybe you're right. But I know someone who'd definitely know."

"Alex," Evan said.

"Alex," Hiram agreed. "What's that other stuff next to it? Is that a symbol?"

Evan stooped down again to get a closer look. A little higher up was another word, this one harder to make out. There was definitely an A, followed by what appeared to be a small 'v'. The next couple of characters were almost undecipherable, but might have been another 'a' and an 'l'. Next was definitely a 'u', followed by what looked like a 'c'. The last character was clearly a 'y'. Again, Evan read them aloud.

"A. V. A. L . U. C. Y. Avalucy? Doesn't make sense."

"Can we remember these letters between us? Maybe the others can work it out."

"I think so," Evan said. "There's also the number nine written multiple times. I'm sure they're single nines too, not ninety-nine, for example. The number nine mean anything to you?"

"Actually, considering who was supposed to have been in these caves, it does."

"Let me guess, you're now going to hit me with hundreds of facts about the Templars, ammiright?"

Hiram grinned. He was well aware he had an innate gift to bore the pants off people by reeling off loads of statistics about things he found fascinating but others... well, to others, much of it was duller than dishwater. "Well, I can see how interested you are, so yes, I will. Okay, the number nine. There were allegedly nine founders of the order original Templar order. There were also allegedly nine provinces of the Temple of the West. It took nine years to lay the foundation of the original Temple of Solomon. I admit the connection gets a little tenuous now, but according to some scholars, there were seventy-two articles to the original Primitive Rule of the Templars."

"Seventy-two?"

"Yes. Well, seven and two. Nine."

"Shit, that is really tenuous."

"Then you'll love this one. Records suggest the Templars were in existence for one-hundred and eighty years."

"One-hundred and eighty. Meaning... one plus eight plus nought equals —"

"Equals nine. See?"

"I do believe you've finally lost it," Evan said, but he couldn't deny he was intrigued. "Any more?"

"Too many to discuss now, but I'll give you one more you'll love. The last Grand Master of the Templars, Jacques de Molay, was apparently executed on March the eighteenth, in the year 1314. Go for it."

Evan frowned, unable at first to see the connection to the number nine. He worked through it slowly. "March eighteenth? March is three. Eighteenth is one and eight. Ignoring March we have one plus eight equals nine."

"Okay... And?"

"The year thirteen fourteen? One, three, one and four. Shit! That's nine too."

"Exactly."

"But what the hell does it mean?"

"It means that if we work out what that second

word means, and find something that relates that to the number nine, then we might just have ourselves a grail quest after all."

"Ha, maybe. But what about those shapes?"

Now it was Hiram's turn to take a closer look. Clutching the slender Maglite torch between his teeth, he dropped to his knees and aimed the torch's beam at the shapes scrawled on the lower area of the stone walls. Now he looked closer, he realised the odd shapes were everywhere. A series of small, concentric squares were dotted around the cave, a shape Hiram knew was often seen in Templar iconography. That part as easy to work out. But the other shape most commonly carved was not obvious. Not obvious at all. It was an animalistic representation of a kind of goat head. Its face was long, and though the torch illuminated the space well enough, the carvings were so old and worn it was difficult to make them out.

What Hiram did know, however, was that representations of goat heads were usually considered to be the antithesis of what the Christian Knights Templar were supposed to follow.

He stood up, his eyes settling on Evan's.

"What is it?" Evan asked. "What d'you see?"

A strange look came over Hiram's face, as if he couldn't quite believe what he'd seen. "Well, mate... I can't be sure. But, if the Templars did once spend time in these caves, and it appears they did... they might very well have been worshipping the devil while they were down here."

"You what? The devil?"

"It appears that way. Those markings seem to me to be representations of Baphomet."

"What or who is Baphomet?"

"Satan."

STOLEN HEART

University of East Anglia, Norwich, United Kingdom
October 4th, 1994

"Sijak," barked the instructor in the Korean language of hanguk. *Begin.*

Hiram Kane bowed slightly, as did the woman stood opposite him on the tae-kwon-do mat. They'd been paired against each other in a pre-tournament sparring bout. Hiram had no qualms about sparring with women — in fact, he sensed he'd have to be at his best in order not to get a hiding from this one.

But during his bow he kept his eyes up, unable to take them off the beautiful woman he was about to spa with. Hiram had seen her around campus a few times over the last few months since the summer break. But as always, when it came to the ladies he never found the courage to speak to them. Tongue tied didn't do his inability to be himself in front of women any justice. He was basically useless.

In fact, Hiram Kane wouldn't know a chat up line if it walked up and punched him on the nose. Despite his appreciation for the fairer sex, Hiram's awkward nature prevented him from making many female friends, and definitely not 'girlfriends'. It was something his best friend Evan never tired of teasing him about. Not that Evan Craft was any better at it than Hiram, but at least he wasn't afraid of trying. In fact, Evan would have made the perfect wingman, if Hiram was just prepared to fly every once in a while. In Evan's case, he flew a lot, but suffered many emergency landings soon after take off.

Both Hiram and the woman stood up from their bows. They each had their eyes fixed on the other's as they slowly circled the mat, waiting for their moment to strike. Then she encouraged him forward. *Shit*, he thought, smiling inwardly. *I'll need to be careful.* Hiram hadn't seen her in the tae-kwon-do class before, but it appeared she knew exactly what she was doing.

The woman — he had no idea what her name was — was tall, at least five-ten, and her long dark hair was tucked beneath a red bandana. Her skin was darker than Hiram's and he guessed she was of

Mediterranean heritage, maybe even Middle-Eastern. He knew nothing at all about her or where she was from. What he did know, however — and without any doubt about it — was that she was the most beautiful woman he'd ever seen.

He sent out a few half-hearted lunges, all which missed by a mile, distracted as he was by the beauty facing him off. Finally he threw a sharp jab, unwilling to be called out for 'going easy' just because she was female. Then, as they continued circling, he thought he heard her whisper, "I'm taking you home tonight."

If it was what she'd actually said or just his imagination playing untimely tricks on him, it completely caught him off guard. It almost cost him a black eye. Noticing his distraction — exactly her intention — she feinted left, then swivelled right and planted a solid right jab on Hiram's right cheek, missing his eye by a fraction. She followed that up with a searing left hook that he only just dodged. As he stumbled back slightly, taken by surprise by the swiftness of the attack, he watched on helpless as the woman shifted her weight onto her right foot, then switched it suddenly back to her left and launched into a spinning roundhouse kick that connected solidly with Hiram's chin and sent him crashing to the mat.

It wasn't a knockout blow, and he sat there stunned, arms behind him and leaning back. The woman stepped closer, her face in shadow beneath the overhead lights.

"My name's Alexandria," she said. She offered her hand.

"Alexandria? My name's Hiram. Hiram Kane. Nice to meet you." Hiram reached out and let Alex help him to his feet.

"I know your name," she replied, stepping once more into a fighting stance. "Friends call me Alex. Let's go again."

And they did. They sparred several more rounds, during which Alex was relentless. Hiram was chivalrous by nature. Yet, if he didn't defend himself and fight back to the best of his ability there might not have been much left in the tank for the tournament bouts by the time Alex was finished with him. They'd both developed a healthy sweat when the instructor finally called a halt to the sparring. They each had a couple of bouts scheduled for the afternoon, and though glad of the rest, Hiram and Alex appreciated the feisty warmup.

After bowing, first to each other, then to the instructor, they stepped off the mat. Turning to Hiram, Alex pulled off her red bandana and unleashed a mane of hair the colour of mahogany. Hiram's eyes opened wide. He wasn't easily wowed, but this was no ordinary woman. Bowled over might have been a more apt phrase. Alex met his gaze, held it for long seconds. Hiram was so enamoured by

Alex's ability and confidence that it inspired his own. He was about to ask her if she might like to go for a cup of tea sometime, when she smiled. With a wink more at home in the Moulin Rouge than beside a university gym mat, she said, "Tae-kwon-do's thirsty work, isn't it? Hanks Bar, eight o'clock. Don't be late."

With that, she was gone. And that was how Hiram Kane first met the woman who would quickly become the love of his life.

"Shit, really? Evan exclaimed as they edged toward the tunnel exit. "But, I thought —"

"... thought Templars were Christians?" Hiram cut in. "Warrior monks sent to the Holy Lands to crusade against all enemies of the Christian church?"

"Uh, yes, something like that."

"And you'd be right. Let's get out of here. As our resident Latin expert and art historian, let's see if Alex can educate us about all things treacherous and satanic."

"There they are," Alex said as she spotted Hiram's head emerge into the daylight. She climbed down off the gate they'd perched on and trotted the thirty yards across the field towards the cave entrance, Luke just steps behind. "Hello boys. What did you find?"

"Are we rich?" Luke asked.

First Hiram then Evan emerged from the small hole in the ground and stood up, stretching a little after being in the cramped tunnel for twenty minutes.

"No, we're not rich," Evan said.

"But we might have found something," Hiram added.

"Really," Alex asked, relieved they were back safely above ground but eager to learn what they'd found.

"Correct me if I'm wrong," Hiram said, "but aren't you a Latin speaking art historian?" He knew Alex was fluent in several languages, and believed Latin was one of them.

"I wouldn't say fluent, but yes, I suppose I'm pretty good at Latin. I'm hardly an art historian yet, either."

"Modest as ever," Hiram said, grinning. He gazed at Alex Ridley now, remembering her beauty was just one of the many reasons he was unashamedly besotted by the multi-talented genius standing before him. "We found some symbols and a few words carved into the stone along the tunnel. One of the words said proditor, with a couple of accent lines above the two Os. Evan thinks it might mean traitor?"

"And he's right. Almost. Proditor is Latin for traitor, but it could also mean Betrayer, which I guess is almost the same thing."

"Interesting. Remember what Steven told us?" Luke said. "He believed the caves were the last hiding place of the Templars." The others nodded their agreement. "Well, what if one of their brethren betrayed their location, gave them up to the Pope or the King's men, something like that? I don't know why, obviously. Maybe as simple as for money?"

"Remember, according to Steven it all started with a 'few flawed men'," Alex said, flashing air quotes.

"And that's why they had to flee?" Evan asked. "So they weren't caught and killed?"

"Yeah. But why were they betrayed?" Luke persisted.

"That's where I think the symbols come in." Hiram explained the stylised Baphomet symbols and the concentric squares.

"Well, you're right about the concentric squares being Templar," Alex told them. "They're found in Templar architecture all across Europe and the Middle-East. As for the Baphomet symbology? Well, it's certainly synonymous with Satan worshipping, but what's that got to do with the Templars?"

"Honestly, I have no idea. But I think we're on the path to finding out."

As Hiram Kane's beloved beige Mini Clubman pulled away from the gate of the remote field in Shropshire, another vehicle eased out from a hidden spot fifty yards behind them. The man driving the sleek black car turned to the man in the passenger seat. He didn't say anything, only looked. The second man acknowledged him with a nod, then both men turned their eyes forward again and onto the Mini in front of them.

This was going to be easier than they'd thought.

STONE #9

It was now three in the afternoon and Evan let it be known in no uncertain terms that it was time to eat and that they should find the nearest pub. No matter how remote the location of the field was, a delightful country pub was never very far away in England.

They soon pulled into The Mason's Arms nearby, parking up and hustling inside just as another flurry of snow fell from ever-darkening winter skies.

They procured a table close to the roaring log fire and ordered a late lunch, including a pint of ale for each of them except Hiram, who refrained as he was driving. They sat chatting for a few minutes until their food came, but conversation dwindled as they all realised how hungry they were and tucked into their meals. Despite being the smallest of them,

Evan's appetite was easily the biggest and he finished a full five minutes before the others.

"So what do you think this means?" he asked, jotting down the letters of the second word they found in the caves on the back of a beer mat.

A. V. A. L . U. C. Y

"Avalucy? That can't be right, can it?" Alex said. "Seven letters. Could be names? Ava and Lucy? They hardly conjure up images of strapping Templar Knights though do they?" The friends chuckled, but it was true.

"I formally declare you Lord Lucy," Evan said. "Rise a Knight... but first take off that skirt." More chuckles followed.

"Could it be a place name?" Luke asked.

"Could be," Evan said, falling serious for a change. "I'm certain the first two letters are A and V, plus the U and the Y are correct. What places can we think of with seven letters?"

"Looks like Aylesbury," Luke said, "but not enough letters."

"What's that place with the stone circle down south?" Evan asked.

"Stone Henge?" Hiram offered.

"No, not Stone Henge, but it's near there I think. Some ancient stone circle thingy, like Stone Henge but —"

"Avebury. You mean Avebury," said the lad from behind the bar, now collecting glasses from the table next to theirs.

The four friends looked at each other, then down at Evan's beer mat. That was it. All eyes fell on Hiram.

"Drink up, my friends… we're going to Avebury."

As promised, Hiram paid everyone's bill while the others went ahead and warmed up the car. He joined them a couple of minutes later. It was now almost dark, the night descending rapidly as winter settled itself in for a couple of months. It meant that by the time they'd driven the hundred and thirty odd miles south to Avebury, down in Wiltshire, it would be about seven in the evening and everything would be closed. Still, if they left now and found a hotel nearby they could get an early start in the morning.

So they headed off . Despite the light snow fall the roads were clear and they made good time, stopping only once for some petrol and a loo break at a garage somewhere on the M5 Motorway.

In the nearby town of Marlborough they easily found a hotel with two spare rooms, one for Hiram and Alex, and Evan and Luke shared a second twin room. After checking in they gathered in the hotel bar, and Hiram procured a round of pints. "We're really only a few miles from the ancient stone circle here," he said. "About half hour drive. Does anyone know anything about it, other than the fact it's really old?"

"Wasn't it built by the druids?" Evan suggested.

"I read a book once that claimed it was built by aliens," chimed in Luke, "as was Stone Henge. Written by Erich von somebody."

"Von Daniken," Hiram said.

"Von what?"

"Erich von Daniken. You're talking about his controversial book from the sixties, Chariots of the Gods. Von Daniken claimed that many of the world's mysterious places... the pyramids, Angkor Wat, Machu Picchu, for example... were all built with the help of ancient aliens, who he claimed we humans are descended from."

"That's ridiculous," Alex said. "No one believes that anymore. Do they?"

"No. Not even Erich himself. But at the time that book, and his others, raised a lot of questions. You have to admit, building some of those ancient monuments must have seemed impossible without some kind of higher technology that humans simply didn't have back then. Most of it's been explained these days, of course, but it was a great book. So, Avebury?"

Luke had snagged a tourist map from the hotel reception and spread it out on the table. "Well, it's a vast complex of stone circles, thought to have been built between four and five-thousand years ago. Damn, that's old."

"Almost as ancient as old man Stalbridge back at the boozer in Nottingham," Evan said, amazing them all once again with his childish humour.

"Look, here's a map of the stones." Luke ran his finger across the map, stopping on the stone marked with the number 9. "Nine was important, wasn't it?"

"Yes, remember I told you that the number nine was significant in Templar history," Hiram, said. "I wonder if that's significant here?"

"Well it seems to me," Evan said, "that's as good a clue as we're going to get. Let's check it out first thing in the morning because... well, what better way to spend the day before Christmas Eve, than traipsing around a snowy field looking at old stones and freezing our bollo —"

"Alright, we get the picture," chided Alex, grinning.

"Hey, I thought you liked my bollo —"

Evan's words were stifled by a wet beer towel slapping round the cheek... expertly aimed by Hiram. Again, more good-natured laughter ensued, except from Evan.

"You lot are so dull," he said, yet, although his voice sounded grumpy the sparkle in his blue eyes betrayed his excitement. "But until then, much more important things are afoot."

"Oh yeah?" Alex asked. "Like what?"

"Like the fact that your boy Kane said drinks were on him on this trip, and my pint's empty."

JUSTICE

After a few pints the friends turned in for the night. Alex and Hiram took the first room, while Evan and Luke shared a twin room at the end of the corridor. Evan had no trouble sleeping anywhere, and was out like a light in seconds. Luke spent thirty minutes reading up on the Avebury world heritage site before eventually succumbing to tiredness.

In the other room, Alex and Hiram lay awake discussing what they'd learned. "But aren't you worried?" Alex asked.

"For our safety? No. I mean, I think we should be careful, of course I do. I don't think anyone's following us or anything. Did you?"

Alex pondered this for a moment. "No... no, I don't." Hiram missed the slight pause. "I don't mean I think there're any crazy bastards out there wanting to kill us or anything." She paused a little longer this time, then offered Hiram a cheeky wink. "But I do think we should consider the fact that there might be other people out there searching for the same thing we are, whatever that might be."

"You're probably right," Hiram conceded, though there had been no evidence of anyone watching them or following. Hiram rolled over and looked at Alex. "It's exciting, isn't it? I mean, all my life I've heard stories about the things my great-grandfather and my grandfather got up to, and ever since I was a kid I've wanted to follow in their footsteps. This is kind of the first real opportunity. Even if nothing comes of it, and I'm well aware it literally is a wild goose chase... well, at least we can say we tried."

"I definitely agree with that. And in the pub Steven seemed so sure we'd find something. I feel kind of responsible to try and find it, if only for him."

"He was very certain, wasn't he? I wouldn't have believed in his story so much had it not been verified by Ian back at St. Giles, either. Between them, they've really got me convinced there's something behind all this. And I only have to ask myself this question to know whether we're doing the right thing or not..."

"What question?" Alex asked, though she thought she knew what it was.

"What would my grandfather do. Whenever I've had big decisions to make in the past, like what course to take at university, which this or which that, if I just put myself in my grandfather's shoes I always seem to make the right choice."

"And what would your grandfather do now?" Alex asked, stretching. She yawned, the day's exertions finally catching up with her.

"Without any shadow of a doubt, he would follow the clues until they led no further, despite any possible risks. He's an adventurer, pure and simple. And I admire him more than any other human I've ever known or probably ever will."

"Any human?" Alex asked and rolled a little closer to Hiram, snuggling into his strong arms.

"Almost any human," he said, welcoming Alex in close.

"Then that's what we shall do too," she said through a yawn. "We'll wake up early, head over to Avebury and see what we can find out for Steven."

"And there's no one I'd rather go on an adventure with than you, Alexandria Ridley. Good night."

Alex was already asleep.

At seven-thirty the next morning Evan awoke with a start. "What the heck?" he said as he shoved his head under the pillow. Then the loud knock on the door was repeated, twice, even louder. Evan groaned, hauled himself out of bed and answered the door.

Standing there with a takeaway cup of steaming

hot tea was a grinning Alex. "Come on Ev, time to go."

Five minutes later they were all in the car and Hiram was easing out of the dark car park, the night still resisting the winter dawn. The roads were deserted, and though the snow had held off, it was bitterly cold. A few minutes later, Hiram pulled the car to a stop outside the visitor car park, which they soon learned didn't open until nine-thirty in the winter months. They left the car parked on the side of the quiet road and headed into the ancient site.

It was no surprise they were all alone. It was barely eight in the morning, barely even light. Most people — the sensible ones — were tucked up warm in their beds enjoying their Christmas holiday lay ins. At least until the shops opened. That's when people headed out, madly hustling around for more useless last-minute Christmas gifts.

"It's this way," Luke said, leading them on. "I mean, I assume we're going to stone number nine?"

"Yes, sir," Hiram said. "That's where we should start."

It was just a couple of minutes' walk until they found themselves standing around the massive, megalithic standing stone number nine.

"Wow, this thing's huge," Evan declared.

"Ah, the man for the understatement," Hiram teased, but Evan was right. "Must be at least ten foot tall."

"Twelve, actually," corrected Luke. "I read it in the guide last night. There's a cool story attached to this stone too. Apparently, many of the stones here at Avebury Henge were buried in the fourteenth-century. The theory is that it came as a result of narrow-minded attempts to de-paganise the site. One day, a pious traveller stopped by and began assisting the Avebury folk to bury the stones. Later, as he was digging out the underside of one of the stones, it toppled over, crushing him to death and burying him beneath it. It became his instant tomb."

"Ooh, nice," Evan said. "What a way to go."

Luke continued. "In nineteen thirty-eight archaeologist Alexander Keiller was on site to shift the stones back into their former positions. During those excavations he discovered the skeleton. A collection of coins found with the body dated it to the early fourteenth-century. Keiller also found and identified a pair of scissors and a medical-looking probe, so he believed the bones belonged to a barber surgeon. There was also a missing arm." Luke paused. "Are you guys with me?"

All three pairs of eyes were on him, and each head nodded. "Well, Keiller sent the remains to the Royal College of Surgeons, where he knew a colleague he thought would appreciate his discovery. His colleague surmised that the man was not killed by the falling megalith, as was believed by the villagers for hundreds of years. In fact, the man was already dead, probably from a loss of blood after…"

"After what?" Alex asked.

"After having his arm hacked off by a blade."

"Let me guess," Hiram said, "a Templar blade?"

"That I don't know. But yes, let's assume it was a Templar sword. It means we're really onto something with all this, doesn't it?"

"I believe it does. Is there a name? I mean, does the skeleton have a name?"

"Actually there is," Luke answered, but didn't offer anything more. Instead he just smiled.

"Well?" Evan said. "Who the hell was it?"

Luke grinned. "Stephen de Stapelbrigg."

"So do we think Mister, uh, Stablehand is —"

"Stapelbrigg."

"Right. Do we think Mister Stapelbrigg is our traitor? The betrayer of Templars?"

"It's starting to look that way," Hiram answered. "But where do we go now?"

"What's that?" Alex asked suddenly, and knelt down at the foot of the huge stone. The day had fully broken now and the flat grassy ground covered in the huge monoliths was bathed in a beautiful, pale yellow glow.

The others crouched down around Alex, hoping to get a better look at what she'd seen.

At the very foot of stone number nine, and partially covered by tufts of grass, was a scratched diagram. Alex pulled away a few clumps of the weedy grass to reveal it better.

"Is that a bird's head, and beak?" Hiram asked. "Looks like it, doesn't it?"

"It does," Luke answered. "But I don't think it is. It's something way cooler than that."

FIRE AT DAWN

"Silbury Hill?" Hiram asked. "Never heard of it."

"Nor had I until last night," admitted Luke. "Apparently it's just a mile down the road. Some kind of ancient man-made burial mound, biggest in Europe by all accounts."

"So, you think the main part of that diagram is the hill? And the, uh, the beak part, is some kind of chamber? Inside the mound?" Alex looked doubtful.

"I don't know, but it certainly looks like that. Think about Egyptian pyramids," Hiram said. "We all know they have chambers built into them, accessed through a series of steep narrow tunnels and passages. Why not here too? Just because this isn't exactly a stone pyramid, it's probably built in a similar way."

"You mean by aliens?" Evan chirped in.

"Yeah, by aliens," Hiram agreed, "your ancestors."

"Can't argue with that," Evan said, and they all chuckled.

"So, shall we head to Silbury Hill," Hiram urged, "see if we aren't just closing in on something pretty damn exciting?"

"Vamanos," Alex said, showing off her Spanish. She remained unconvinced, but like the others she was keen to check it out anyway.

The four of them headed away from the impressive monolith beneath the rising glow of the sun and angled back to the road beyond the car park.

What they saw when they got there froze them all in their tracks.

Hiram's beloved Mini, the first and only car he'd ever owned, was on fire. Not just a few flames gusting from the engine either. In the pale lemon tinged dawn, it resembled a scene from an action movie. The small car was burning like a conflagration, flames and sparks and thick black smoke swirling up into the clear morning sky.

"What the fuck?" Evan yelled.

"My God," muttered Alex.

Luke managed, "Jesus, how the hell did that happen?"

Only Hiram was silent. In fact, his momentary shock had already passed, his eyes now focused on the surrounding area, scanning for any people nearby. He didn't see any, but he did spot a dark car parked far away down the road. It was the only other vehicle anywhere in sight. It wasn't there when they'd arrived, he was certain of that. It wasn't moving. It was just parked there, facing them. As if whoever was inside was… watching…

"What the hell happened?" Evan shouted. "How did it just… spontaneously combust?"

"I've never seen anything like it," Alex agreed.

"This was no accident," Hiram declared, his voice surprisingly calm.

"Wait, what?" Luke said, incredulous. "What do you mean, no accident?"

"Exactly what I said. Someone did this on purpose."

"Who? Who the hell would do this?" Evan asked, now thoroughly concerned, his eyes skitting about frantically .

"They did." Hiram's arm raised slowly and pointed down the road. All eyes followed until they rested on the black car parked a couple of hundred yards away. "It was them."

"But… how do you know?" Alex's voice was far from calm.

"There's no one else here, Alex. And I'm certain they're watching us right now."

"What do we do? Are we safe? We should call the police!" Evan acted tough sometimes, yet he was much more likely to run away than fight, usually the sensible option.

"We can't call the police, Ev."

"Why the hell not? Of course we can, and we should."

"Do you see a phone box anywhere? If there is one, it'll be at the tourist office the other side of the site. To get there, we'd have to go past them."

Hiram had made a solid argument. There weren't any phone boxes around, and in the days before the advent of mobile phones there was simply no way to make the call.

"Well we can't just stand here and do nothing. So what'll we do?"

Unlike Evan, Hiram was always the first to get stuck in when witnessing almost any kind of injustice. It wasn't that he liked fighting. It's just that he was good at it. Ever since his brother Danny had gone missing some eleven years previous – in an event Hiram had felt guilty about ever since – he'd carried that guilt around his neck like a penance, which often manifested itself in a physical way. Usually it was reserved for a genuine outlet, like representing his university on the rugby field, in which he was an outstanding full back. Other times it was when he pushed himself extra hard in the gym, or running a dozen miles instead of the planned six.

Sometimes though, just sometimes, that guilt morphed into a helpless rage. It took a lot for it to emerge, but when it did it was a sight to behold. It was why he had taken up tae-kwon-do classes in the first place. The Korean martial art was all about focus and discipline, not violence. Hiram had needed to rely on those disciplines numerous times when out and about; drunken idiots starting pointless fights; bullies pushing their wives or girlfriends around; a big guy picking on a smaller one to show off to his mates. Hiram had seen it all, and he would never, ever stand by and do nothing.

And as he stood there now, his beloved car a flaming wreck and his close friends now worried for their safety, that rage began bubbling to the surface. It rose slowly at first. But with each passing second it rose further, until eventually the red mist descended and he set off in a sprint. His long, powerful legs pounded the tarmac and ate up the distance towards the black car. He was unable to hear the warning cries of his friends as he flew towards it, determined to find out who it was that had destroyed his car and scared his closest friends, ready to mete out his own form of justice.

Sitting in the car, the two men turned to each other. They watched on, faces passive, as the tall guy stared at them from beside the burning car. Next they watched as he suddenly burst into a dead run directly toward them. With narrowed eyes and the hint of a grin, the man in the passenger seat nodded. The driver returned the nod, amusement in his eyes.

Then he put the car into first gear, and spun the wheel hard, steering the car in a U-Turn and accelerating away down the road, leaving Hiram Kane closing in on where they had parked.

Hiram stopped, leant over and placed his hands on his knees. In the cold air, his breaths came in warm bursts, misting in front of him. Despite leaning over, he kept his head up and never took his eyes from the car as it spun away and sped off, the roar of the engine destroying the silence of the otherwise peaceful dawn.

Eventually, he turned and walked back to his friends, who had started along the road and met him half way. "I don't know who the hell they are, but they've seriously pissed me off."

"Who might they've been?" Evan asked. He was sorry Hiram's car was a wreck, but glad they'd left before Hiram reached them. Although, he wasn't sure who was the luckiest, his mate or the fuckers in the car.

"I don't know. My best guess is that they overheard our conversation with Steven in the pub. Listen, I don't think they want to hurt us. They probably just want to scare us off, encourage us to leave this all alone."

"Well maybe we should," Alex said. "I mean, we don't even know what it is we're looking for. It might be nothing. So if it's nothing, why don't we let them have it? Right?"

Hiram nodded. "You're probably right. We should leave it alone. You guys should head back to the hotel, or to the nearest bus stop. Head home. I have money for your tickets."

"Wait a minute," Luke said, his brow furrowed. "You're leaving too, right?"

Hiram nodded again. "Yes, of course I'm leaving." He paused, his expression serious. "But not yet."

SINK OR SWIM

"What do you mean, not yet?" Alex said. "We have to leave now. We must."

"With respect Alex," he said, grabbing her hands in his, "I didn't come all this way to be put off by some idiots in a shiny black car. You guys should go. It might be dangerous now, so you —"

"Do you remember that time down at Fisher's Row? Back when we were kids?" Evan asked, cutting his friend off. He took a deep breath, his eyes narrowing. Hiram turned to face his oldest friend. He did remember. He would never forget it.

They were just eight years old. Hiram and Evan were fishing on the River Waveney, on the muddy bank at Fisher's Row at a place known locally as Camp's Heath. Hiram was useless at fishing, much to Evan's amusement. Neither was he a strong swimmer back in those days. The boys larked about as they always did, daring each other to walk along the manmade wooden banks, acting as if they were gymnasts on a beam. After each successful pass, their moves got more daring. That was, until Hiram attempted an unlikely handstand. He fell backwards into the fast-flowing water. Under the dark surface he went, his legs tangling in the submerged fronds of the stonewort plant. He panicked, arms and legs thrashing, and with each flail of a limb their grip tightened. He held his breath, but it was no use. His eyes dimmed as blackness crept into the edges of his vision. Hiram was about to succumb when he felt himself hauled from beneath the surface and shoved over to the river bank.

Without a second's hesitation, Evan had dived in to save his friend. It was the memory of that terrifying experience, the scariest event of his life at that time, why he knew there was no way on earth he could convince Evan to leave him now.

"Yeah, I remember. Fair enough. But Alex, and Luke... you two should go. It might not be safe for you —"

"Do I look like a woman who's scared of a little danger?" Alex said, and stepped closer. "Might I remind you I once kicked your arse on the tae-kwon-do mat. So, you need me here. I'm staying." Hiram could only grin at that.

With Alex and Evan demonstrating their bravery, Luke suddenly felt even more scared. This wasn't him, not at all what he was about. Not what he was about at all. He was a student. A self-confessed nerd. But he didn't want to seem as if he was a chicken. Luckily Hiram noticed, and quickly saved his blushes.

"Luke, we'll need another car. Could you do us a favour and head to the information booth at the tourist centre?" He looked at his watch. "It's almost nine. The tourist office probably opens soon, and they'll be able to tell you where the nearest place is to rent a car. Would you do that for us?"

Internally Luke was relieved, if not a little ashamed. "Uh, yeah, sure. I can do that. If you're sure you don't need me to come with you?"

"Absolutely. We need to get out of here. Also, we need someone to know where we've gone, you know, just in case something happens. I'm sure it won't."

"Okay," Luke said quietly. "If you insist."

"I do." Luckily hadn't left his wallet in the car. Flipping it open, he handed Luke some cash. They arranged to meet at the Silbury Hill car park in two hours. They figured that would be enough time for Luke to locate a rental car, and for Hiram and the others to make their way to Silbury Hill.

Maybe there they would find out just what the hell was going on.

ONE GIANT STEP

"Well, be bloody careful alright," Luke said as he set off up the road.

"Don't worry, I'll keep the boys in order." Alex grinned, though she now shared Hiram's anger.

"Good luck finding us a car, buddy," Hiram said. Once Luke was out of sight, his long legs angling across the ancient World Heritage site towards the tourist hut, Hiram turned and looked pointedly at his friends. Aside from his immediate family members, they were the two people he cared most about on the planet. "Listen, I know I'd be wasting my time asking you to leave. I'm going to anyway. Please go now, and catch up with Luke. It might not be safe."

"You said that already. We already said we're going with you," Evan told him.

"I honestly don't think there'll be any trouble," said Alex, though she wouldn't have minded if there was. She was as tough as Hiram... if not tougher. "My guess is that whoever these bastards are that wrecked your car, they already know what it is we're looking for. They just want to deter us. There's probably nothing actually there in terms of... I don't know, and I know this sounds ridiculous... but you know... treasure. I'm sure it's just a place, some kind of secret location they don't want people snooping around."

Hiram nodded. "I'm inclined to agree with you. I'm still going. And if you're coming with me, let's get on with it."

With that Hiram, Alex and Evan headed off in the opposite direction to Luke, but Hiram paused to take one last look at his pride and joy, his Mini Clubman. "Meh, she was getting old anyway. I've been thinking of getting something newer."

"Let's be honest," Evan said as they continued moving away, "you can bloody well afford it. What're you going to get? A Porsche?"

"A Porsche? Me? No chance. I was thinking of getting another... Mini. Wouldn't get anything else if you paid me."

Evan groaned, but he'd always known Hiram was never one to flash his money around on something as mundane as a car. Despite his relative wealth, Hiram was definitely the least materialistic person Evan knew, an admirable quality he didn't quite share.

"And there's plenty of room in a Mini," Alex said, "for, you know —"

"Alright, alright, I get it," Evan said, "Minis are great. Let's get the hell out of here."

They left the ancient site of Avebury and had soon located the footpath Luke had told them about that ran south alongside the River Kennet. They edged past a small stand of weeping willows, their yellow leaves dangling just above the slow-flowing river. Then into their view came their first glimpse of the impossibly huge Silbury Hill. It towered above the surrounding landscape, and seemed so out of place it was as if they'd been transported to another world. Luke had told them it was the largest manmade mound in Europe. It was easy to see why.

"Wow, that's amazing," declared Alex. "I had no idea there was anything like this in England, did you?"

"I knew there were huge mounds," Hiram answered, "like the ones beneath Nottingham and Norwich castles, for example. But this is way bigger than those. Unreal."

"Let me guess... aliens?" Evan chirped in, though he too was suitably impressed.

"No," Hiram said, "just a load of subjugated people with spades, I reckon, being forced to worship either the sun or the moon, or a load of scary men with whips."

They trampled on along the winding path, the river flowing gently below the bank. The sun still shone to the east, but thick clouds had rolled in slowly from the west, clouds that looked as if they might dump a load of snow at any moment and cover the green, iconic rolling fields of England that stretched out either side of the river. Green or white, England had a unique beauty all of its own. There was no time to enjoy that now. It was cold, and getting colder. Bone-achingly cold. They had to move on.

Fifteen minutes and one mile later they had left the river side and skirted across the field. A minute after that they stood at the foot of the massive mound, craning their necks to gaze up at it from below. Just then snow started to fall in large, drifting flakes.

"Great," Evan whined, "just what we need."

"I don't imagine there's a door," Hiram said drily. "Why don't we split up and walk in opposite directions around the base, see what we can find?"

"Yep, good idea," Alex agreed. "Ev, you and I will go this way, and you go that way. Meet you round the other side?"

"Okay, let's go. And Alex... be careful."

Alex nodded, and grabbing Evan's arm she led him off clockwise around the base of the huge mound that was slowly being blanketed in pristine white snow.

Five minutes later they met up again, this time on the far side of the hill. "Man, this thing is massive, isn't it?"

"Kind of the understatement strikes again. Did you find anything?" asked Hiram. He hadn't, and doubted the others had either.

"No, afraid not. So what do we do?" Alex doubted they'd find anything. "If the Templars did use this place for some kind of secret hideout, there's no way us amateurs will find it." She looked at Hiram, an uneasy feeling washing over her as she saw the strange look in his eye. She's seen that look before, right before he'd dived off a cliff in Greece from a height that made her knees go weak just thinking about it. You could say what you wanted about Hiram Kane, but you couldn't ever call him a chicken shit. "What're you thinking?"

"Amateur huh? he said, feigning hurt.

"You know what I mean."

He nodded. "Well there's nothing down here, is there?"

"No. And –"

"And if there's anything to find down here, then it must be up there. See ya."

And with that, Hiram began scrambling up the steep snow-covered grassy flank of Silbury Hill. He slowly placed one foot above the other in the snow and, digging his toes into the soft earth beneath, he hauled himself up with his strong arms.

"Hiram, wait!" she yelled. "It's too slippery... you'll fall."

But Hiram was gone. Within seconds he was

twenty-feet above them, scrambling up like some kind of mountain goat. Evan looked at Alex, an almost hopeless look on his face that she understood.

"Well, he *is* Hiram Kane... if you can't beat join, join him." A second later, Evan took a deep breath and began scrambling up the side of the hill too. Hiram had veered off to the right, as well as up, so Evan veered left, essentially widening the search.

Down below, Alex rolled her eyes. Sometimes it was like babysitting with these two. Then again, she wouldn't have it any other way. She eased around the base of the hill, keeping one eye on Hiram and the other on Evan. "Be careful," she called up in vain, but there came no reply. She guessed Hiram was focused on his footing. It was a long way down, and though the ground was soft beneath the now two inch-thick layer of snow and the thick, tufty grass, if he fell he would surely break something.

Up above, Hiram concentrated hard on placing his feet. He didn't even really know what he was looking for. Yet, he felt sure there was a hidden entrance of some kind somewhere near the top of what was essentially a manmade pyramid.

Round the other side of the mound Evan was doing the same. "One small step for me," he said, "one small step for —"

His foot slipped and his body slid from under him, slamming his face into the icy snow. Luckily, his hands had a good grip on the clumped grass beneath the snow and he managed to arrest his slide before it was too late. "Fuck! Take it slowly dude," he muttered, and continued on.

Three minutes later, Evan and Hiram emerged into each others' view and came to a stop close together. "Anything?" Hiram asked, though he already knew the answer.

"Nothing. You?"

"Nothing. Dammit, I felt sure there'd be something. How the hell did they get in?"

"Dunno," Evan answered, "but I think we should get down."

"Agreed. Be careful, okay, wouldn't want you to face-plant the snow."

Evan grimaced in agreement but said nothing. He was *not* about to admit it and give Hiram banter fodder.

A couple of nervous minutes later, both men had made it safely down to ground level again. There was no sign of Alex. "Alex? Where'd you go?"

No answer. A knot of fear came unbidden into Hiram's guts. "Alex? Come on, where are you?"

Hiram's voice grew frantic, and Evan knew immediately it wasn't just because he was worried for Alex. He had known Hiram back when his brother Danny went missing from the Old Rectory when they were just kids. He also knew Hiram had always blamed himself for Danny's disappearance. The truth was, no one knew what had actually happened to his little brother. He simply vanished. There was no sign of any struggle, no evidence as to where he was or where he might have gone. No body.

Over the years, the family eventually accepted that something terrible had happened to Danny. Every day since, Hiram had accepted that it was all his fault. He had coerced his brother to go with him to the abandoned Old Rectory that day, skipping school and breaking in to the derelict, crumbling building. It was his fault, and as long as he lived he would never get over it.

"Alex, please, where —"

"Hey boys, what took you so long?"

"Alex? Where were you? I was wo —"

"Over there. I found something you're going to want to see."

INTO THE BREACH

"Unbelievable." It wasn't Hiram's most eloquent response. It was valid none the less.

Alex had led them away from the enormous mound and back towards a small branch of the river, that angled away from the main flow and back towards the mound. Then it curved back and rejoined the river again a hundred yards further south.

"But... how did you know?" Evan asked, equally as amazed as Hiram.

"The etching on stone nine back at Avebury. Remember how Luke said it looked like some kind of stylised bird's head? There was also that ribbony thing that looked a little like a worm. I thought about it and wondered if it might not have been that at all, but instead I figured it might just be a tunnel. There were also those wavy scratches carved into the stone too, which I guessed might be water. And here I am." Alex grinned and spread her arms out, indicating the unlikely scene before them.

They were standing below a small cliff at the edge of the shallow branch of the river. It was impossible to see from any distance away. From either side it just looked as though it were a naturally undulating part of the landscape. However, what looked like a man-made gulley was cut through the terrain around that stretch of the river. Within the north side bank, a small entrance had been dug right into the cliff face. The two-foot square hole was covered by a set of seriously strong-looking bars, in case anybody happened to stumble upon it. If they did — which did seem unlikely — they'd probably just think it was some kind of sewage system, maybe even irrigation for the nearby fields. Anyone without the naturally curious mind of Alex Ridley might simply have ignored it and walked on. Not Alex.

"I think we've found our entrance," she said. "But how about these bars? Wouldn't we be breaking and entering?"

"We would," Hiram agreed. "I won't tell anyone if you won't"

Diminutive in stature, Evan was wiry and strong. With Alex keeping watch, he and Hiram made short work of the metal grate covering the entrance. In fact, Hiram felt as if it were too easy, almost as if it'd recently been opened.

The last thing he wanted to do was put Evan or Alex in any unnecessary danger. Yet, he knew there was simply no way he could convince them not to follow him inside. Besides, Alex was a match for anybody in a one-on-one fight. Equally, Evan's tenacity and sinewy strength more than made up for his slight frame. The three of them together were a formidable team. He only hoped they wouldn't have to prove it.

Keeping his unease to himself for now, Hiram dropped to his knees and eased his body through the small entrance. He was closely followed by Evan. After a final, furtive look around, and confident the coast was clear, Alex dropped down too and scurried through the entrance. She pulled the grate closed behind her.

Once inside a few yards, they weren't surprised to find the earthen walls of the tunnel lined with ancient-looking oil lamps. It seemed none had been lit recently, based on an absence of any lingering scent of burned oil. Nevertheless, that didn't mean no one had been through there lately. Again, Hiram felt uneasy. He got the distinct impression that in fact someone had been. Recently. With a deep breath, both to steel his nerves and sharpen his focus, he turned and led his friends further along the passage way.

The tunnel sloped up initially, which Hiram believed was to help prevent flooding when the river was high. Then it gradually sloped down again, and curved away to what he felt was north, directly towards the looming bulk of Silbury Hill.

After five minutes of moving along the trail, the passage widened into what was more of a subterranean chamber. Hiram's Maglite did little to counter the darkness, but gave just enough of a glow to lead the way and keep them from stumbling.

What they saw next didn't really come as a surprise either. Shining the torch onto the earthen wall facing them, they saw a series of icons carved into the surface. Once again they saw the concentric square imagery synonymous in Templar iconography. Many examples of it decorated the chamber, but they paled into insignificance when the torch illuminated what was clearly the centrepiece of the display. Hiram and Evan had seen something similar on the walls of the cave back at Caynton in Shropshire. But those were scuffed and almost worm smooth from centuries of wear.

Not this one. There before them on the wall, approximately six foot in diameter, was a huge rendering of the Baphomet icon. Set within two concentric circles and inter-crossed with a pentagon, it immediately brought to mind Leonardo Da Vinci's famous Vitruvian Man symbol. Yet, it also had connotations with Satanic rituals and devil worshipping. It made them all stop in their tracks.

"Alright," Evan whispered, "what the hell is this place?"

"I do believe we've stumbled upon something very Templar," Alex said. "Look, there... That creepy image does appear to be some kind of satanic symbol, but it isn't. Traditionally, the pentagon is used to ward off evil spirits. Over the centuries its meaning somehow has been lost in translation."

"What about the goat?" Evan asked. "Goats are evil. I've seen it with my own eyes."

Hiram chuckled, but quickly stifled it. "It's like we discussed earlier. Many people believed the Templars worshipped the devil, but that was just a smear campaign by the Pope at the time to turn the people against the Templars. He was both jealous of their enormous wealth, and concerned about their growing power because of it. It worked, too. Ultimately it led to the massacre on Friday the thirteenth."

"Hiram's right. The goat is also considered evil in some cultures, but in many others it's a symbol of vitality and health. They can't help it if they've got creepy eyes, can they? And anyway, how do you know goats are evil? What did you do wrong?"

"That's a story for another day," Evan said, winking.

"Anyway, it seems we're in the right place," Hiram said. "Shall we go on?"

DEEP FREEZE

Luke had waited patiently at the entrance to the Avebury Historic Monument's Visitor Centre. At exactly nine o'clock, an elderly lady approached the door from the inside. With an amused look on her face, she slid back the bolts, undid the lock and opened up the door.

"Good morning, young man," she said. "Have you been waiting long?"

"No, no, not really. Half an hour maybe?"

"Half an hour? Whatever for? You can visit the monuments without a ticket you know."

"Yes, I know. It's, well... I..." Luke simply didn't know what to say. Hiram had said earlier they couldn't tell the police, but that was only because the mysterious men in the car had blocked the path to the nearest phone. There was no sign of that car, nor those two men, anywhere in sight. So, should he tell the staff here? Should he call the police? In the end he figured that the ladies working in this tourist centre would only tell him to call the police anyway, and the police were likely some distance away in the nearest town, probably Marlborough where they'd stayed last night. His instinct was to say nothing and do what he had been asked to do by Hiram; locate the nearest car rental place, rent a car, and meet them back at Silbury Hill. So that's what he did.

After asking her about a car rental, the lady informed him that the nearest place was indeed in nearby Marlborough. Luke knew that was too far to walk. However, if he stuck around until nine thirty the first tourist bus from the town would arrive and he could hop on for the ride back. With little choice but to wait, he did. Luke wasn't known for his patience at the best of times. Yet, with his nerves frazzled and his mind conjuring up all sorts of images of burning cars, crazed robed figures in ancient caves, and —

Something caught his attention from of the corner of his eye. He spun to look out of the window. Just fifty yards away and facing directly at the visitor centre was the same black car that had been watching them earlier. It wasn't moving, but Luke could hear its engine running. *What the heck?* He couldn't see, but he suspected the same two men from earlier were watching, trying to figure out where Hiram and his friends were. If they saw Luke alone, they might guess the others had gone on to Silbury Hill. He didn't want to be the one responsible for giving away that information. That was, if they didn't already assume that. Luke realised there was no way they could've made out who was in the building from that distance. So, they probably believed all the friends were still together. He drew in a deep breath and ducked a little further away from the window behind a display of maps and flyers.

His mind swirled in a maelstrom of uncomfortable questions. Who the hell are these men? What are they after? Are they dangerous? Do they work for some shady organisation? Luke had read enough books and seen enough movies that he knew he was probably being paranoid. But... Well, you just never knew. He'd been terrified when Hiram had gone sprinting toward the car to confront the men. That was either incredibly brave or incredibly stupid. Luke figured it was probably both. There was no way he was going to do the same.

Luke was just about to ask if there was another way out of the visitor centre, when the car spun around and sped off in the opposite direction, tyres squealing loud enough to cause the lady behind the counter to offer up a couple of audible tuts.

"Youngsters today," she said, then added, "I mean, some youngsters. You're obviously a fine upstanding young man." She blushed a little. Luke forced a smile.

Fifteen minutes later the tourist bus pulled up and stopped in the parking bay across the road from the visitor centre. A dozen or so brightly-clothed tourists clambered off, followed by the driver, who lit up a cigarette. He took a few swift puffs, and less than thirty seconds later he jumped back aboard. Luke took that as his cue to leave. He thanked the lady, trotted over to the bus, paid for his ticket and was soon zooming through the countryside to Marlborough, almost nauseous with worry about his friends down at Silbury Hill.

Luke had been right. It was the same black car. He was wrong about one thing; the men had seen it was only Luke inside, and assumed the others had already headed off to Silbury Hill. So they turned the car around and headed the half mile along the Beckhampton Road, took a sharp left east on the A4, and just a minute later pulled into the deserted car park at Silbury Hill.

The two men climbed out of the car and hurried round to the back. Lifting the boot, they unzipped a large black holdall and, looking around, each man took out one item and stowed it beneath their dark jackets. The driver quietly closed the lid of the boot and both men strode with purpose through the empty car park. Their heavy boots crunched through the snow-covered gravel until, just a few minutes later, they were following three fresh sets of footprints in the snow down to the narrow branch of the River Kennet.

The tunnel had become a chamber. Now though there had been another significant change. The earthen walls had been replaced entirely by stone. In the darkness they couldn't tell if it was simply stone cladding on top of the earth behind, or if it was actually a chamber carved out of the natural bedrock. That seemed unlikely to Hiram. For humans to have created this massive earthen mound — the largest in Europe — was impressive enough. For it to have been built around some kind of granite rock formation, then carved from the inside out, seemed improbable at best, if not impossible.

Due to his studies on the archaeology modules of his degree, he knew humans were capable of extraordinary feats of engineering. He had visited many of the finest and most amazing examples himself. That included world famous Machu Picchu in Peru on a visit with his grandfather when he was a teenager. And yet, although magnificent Stone Henge was just down the road, and Avebury itself literally around the corner, Hiram didn't think this was as technologically advanced as those legendary manmade wonders of the ancient world.

One more thing really made them pay attention.

Rather than just a series of shabby oil lamps attached to the walls of the initial chamber, now there were a series of elaborate natural torches. They remained unlit. Each was encased in a carved holder made of some sort of... was that bone?

"That's bone," Hiram declared. "Jesus, what the hell is this place?"

Despite his torch, it was still incredibly dark in the chamber and Hiram had to put his face right up to one of the torches on the wall to get a good enough look. He surmised the holders were indeed carved from ivory.

"This is no simple cave system," he said. "This is starting to look very much like a temple."

"A Templar, uh, temple?" Evan asked, as blown away by their surroundings as Hiram.

"I believe so, yes." He turned to Alex. "What do you make of it?"

"I think you're right. You're the resident Templar expert, but those markings... the concentric squares we've seen already over the last couple of days... are definitely related to Templar iconography. So yes, I think we can safely say we're in a Templar —"

"Freeze! Stop right there! Nobody move!"

FIRE IN THE HOLE

Hiram, Alex and Evan hadn't seen the men coming. Hadn't even heard them.

The two men were standing behind them dressed entirely in black and with dark hats pulled low over their eyes. The only thing showing were the whites of their eyes.

Their eyes, and the two large guns that glistened black beneath the glow of Hiram's torch.

"Who are you?" asked one of the men. His low voice remained calm, though the origin of his accent was unclear. "What you doing here?"

Nobody answered. They were each stunned to find themselves staring down the barrels of two guns.

"He asked who you are? And why you here?" said the other man. He was taller than the first, thicker set, and this time Hiram sensed a hint of a

Middle-Eastern accent, possibly North African in the fractured English.

"My name's Hiram. And honestly, I don't know why we're here." Hiram sensed he should be cautious, probably frightened. After all, there were two guns just several feet from his head. Yet it wasn't in his nature to be afraid. Not in his nature at all. He wasn't scared of any man, and his few years of tae-kwon-do training had equipped him with some pretty dangerous fighting moves. But he fought to calm his fighting instincts, urging himself not to react in his natural way. Which would have been to throw himself straight at the nearest man and take him down with a couple of swift and crippling kicks to the head. But it might have been a suicide mission. He was not going to put Alex and Evan's lives in more danger than they might already be in. He took a few deep breaths, then said, "Might I ask who you are?"

"No, you might not," said the first man, shorter than the other but with solid shoulders. "Who we are matters little. What we want to know..."

"What we demand," chimed in the second man.

"... is why you are here."

"Like I said, I honestly don't know. Exploring?"

The man stepped forward so fast Hiram didn't have time to avoid the fist that smashed into his jaw. It rocked his head back, but it wasn't a knockout blow. Nobody knocked Hiram Kane out. He grabbed at his jaw and shook his head. He checked his fingers for blood. Seeing none, he lowered his hand. He took another deep breath and rose to his full height, defiance in his eyes stirred by anger.

"I ask one more time. Why you here?"

Hiram had to think fast. Whoever they were, it seemed as if these guys didn't really know why they were there. That meant they probably didn't know what was there inside Silbury Hill either. Hmm...

Hiram took a chance. "You know why we're here. The same reason you are."

The two men glanced at each other. Hiram couldn't be sure, but he thought he saw a flicker of confusion pass between them. In the darkness he was far from certain. A long moment of silence ensued, during which the only thing Hiram heard was the blood thundering through his own temples. Finally the man spoke.

"You are right. We are here for same reason as you. But I have gun. So, friend, it is you who will lead way."

"We are not friends," Hiram spat, pissed off that he was powerless against two cowardly fuckers with weapons.

"So be it. Not friends," the man said. "But you will do what I say, or woman will feel wrong end of gun."

Hiram tensed, and it took all his inner strength to stop himself launching at the scumbag with the gun. He turned to Alex, unsurprised to see defiance etched onto her face. She was as brave as any person he'd ever met. There was no better ally to have alongside him if it came down to hand-to-hand combat. Sadly, these bastards had guns.

Evan on the other hand was not so defiant. He remained silent. His expression screamed fear. He had backed away slowly, and now was hard up against the stone wall of the chamber.

"I said lead way," barked the shorter man. "Now!"

Hiram's eyes narrowed even more. Mr fucking Napoleon syndrome, he thought as he looked around. His torch was weak, and though his eyes had grown more accustomed to the darkness, there seemed to be no obvious way out of the chamber.

"As you can see," he said defiant, "this is a dead end. In fact, we were just about to turn around and go right back the way we came from." His voice was calm, but his heart rate had notched up a couple of levels, not from fear but from the ever-growing mix of helplessness and rage.

The two men looked at each other again, unconvinced by Hiram's words. They simply didn't believe him. "Last chance. Go. Now!"

Hiram was now seriously worried. There was no way out he could see, only the way they'd arrived from. "Look around you. Can't you see there's no way out of here except behind you?"

"He's right," Alex said, her voice as calm as if she were on a stroll in the countryside. "Take a look... there's nowhere to go." She waved her arms around the stone chamber, demonstrating the lack of any obvious passage way out of there.

The two men were becoming increasingly frantic. The first man actually ripped off his hat, revealing a shock of jet black hair that spilled to his shoulders. "It can not be," he said. "Where is inner temple? I demand you take me to inner temple now!"

It was Hiram's turn to display his confusion. Inner temple? Had they really discovered a secret Templar temple? He couldn't believe it. "I promise, I don't know what you're talking about. I —"

The single gunshot sounded more like a bomb in the enclosed space as it slammed into the rock above Evan's head, showering them all in a barrage of stone fragments and dust. Evan screamed and fell to his knees as the report of the gunshot reverberated around the chamber.

No one was hurt. Yet things had just become a whole lot more serious. "This is last chance. Where is fucking inner temple? Tell me now. Or she dies!"

Hiram's heart skipped several beats. He didn't know anything about any inner temple. What could he tell them? Just lie? Try buying them some time? But who was going to come and help them? Only

Luke knew roughly where they were, and he was going to be waiting in the car park.

With his blood boiling, his nerves shredded and with no better choice presenting itself, he did the thing that seemed most natural

Hiram Kane attacked.

NEO TEMPLARS?

It looked certain the big man with the gun was about to shoot Alex, so Hiram launched himself into a *Twim-yo Yeop Chagi*... a flying side kick. It happened in a blur. Hiram's momentum and innate power crashed his lead foot into the man's chest, slamming him unceremoniously back against the stone wall just as Hiram landed with the grace of a gymnast. The other guy... the stumpy Napolean... had barely reacted by the time Hiram turned his attention to him. The man's gun was on the rise and Hiram was about to unleash a *Doll-yeo Chagi*... a roundhouse kick... when from out of nowhere two more shadowy figures emerged. In less than two seconds, in a whirl of white material and glinting blades, the remaining gunman was incapacitated and pinned to the floor. Two further seconds resulted in both guns being removed their and neither aggressor able to move a single muscle.

Shocked, Alex scurried back against the wall, no idea what was happening. Hiram stepped back in front of her, certain they were about to be attacked by these new characters and desperate to protect his love. A few seconds of quiet followed. The new men moved swiftly, paying no attention to Hiram and his friends. Instead, they set about the restraining the thugs dressed in black, until a few seconds later they turned to face Hiram, side by side, unspeaking.

Seconds passed, then a few more. The attack Hiram feared never came. Everything had fallen silent. After a full minute, one of the men finally spoke. "Do not fear us."

Hiram sensed more than saw he could believe the man's words. The man nodded, then they both turned and set about lighting several of the naked-flame torches on the walls, a surreal, flickering glow about the chamber. The two new men stood there calmly, each next to one of the fallen men, and each resting on a huge, glimmering sword. They were big men, huge in fact and bigger than the original assailants. Hiram didn't sense any danger from these new men. If anything, he thought he might have even spotted a trace of amusement in their eyes.

"Good morning," one of them said. "And who might you be?"

Hiram Kane wasn't known for his eloquence, and

liked to consider himself a man of action rather than words. But he had never before been rendered totally speechless. He was now, and simply stared at the two huge men before him.

"Don't be afraid. We're not going to hurt you," said the other man. "But we'll be more likely to if you don't tell us who you are, and how you came to be here. So please, tell us who you are."

Hiram tried to speak, but no words came. Alex helped him out.

"We are... Well, we aren't anybody really. We heard a story about some... um, some Templar history. We wanted to check it out. You know... For a friend. We kind of stumbled across this place." It was more or less true.

"For a friend, huh? And who might this friend be?" The man's eye had a definite glint, almost as if he knew the answer before hearing it.

Alex didn't know whether to answer truthfully or not. Like Hiram, she didn't feel any threat from these men. She glanced at Hiram now, who seemed as confused as she felt. He offered her the slightest shrug, as if to say, *why not?* She decided to tell the truth.

"We met a guy in a pub. An old guy, big, like you..."

"And where might this pub have been? Let me guess... far away from here?"

Alex looked once more at Hiram. He shrugged again. "Yes, pretty far away."

Evan was up on his haunches now, sensing he might not actually die there today after all.

The man smiled. "And if I was to say Nottingham, would I be getting warm?"

"Yes. How did... how did you know?" Alex said, barely able to get the words out. This was getting more and more weird by the minute.

"Listen, by now you've worked out this is somewhere you're not supposed to be. However, since you've made it this far, and since we don't think you're any kind of threat, why don't we give you the grand tour?"

Hiram simply couldn't believe what he was hearing. *Are these men... Templars? For real?* It didn't make any sense. He had heard of organisations that claimed to be remnants of the Templars. They were often right-wing, nationalist groups who used their alleged Christian affiliations to campaign against things like immigration and other non-Christian religions. But these men? They didn't seem like that at all. Could they possibly be descended from real Templar Knights? How could he know? Hiram felt ridiculous even thinking it. But that's how it seemed.

He stepped forward, as did Alex. More reluctantly, Evan finally unfurled himself from his corner and came to stand beside them. "I guess so," Hiram said. "I mean... Yes, that would be great."

The man smiled again. "Very good. Let us deal with these people first." He glanced up at something unseen by Hiram and the others, and a moment later two more men stepped into view from what must have been a carefully concealed entrance into the chamber. The two new men grabbed the restrained attackers under their armpits, and dragged them out of sight the same way they'd entered.

"They're not, uh, dead are they?" Evan asked, the first words he'd spoken in ages.

The two men shared a look, a message passing between them. The older of the two answered. "Let's just say they're out of action for a while. Believe it or not, not all Templars enjoy slaying the enemy. Nice move by the way," he added, nodding at Hiram. "Impressive."

"So who are they?" Alex asked.

"Before we get into that, let me introduce myself. My name's James, and this is my brother, John. Why don't you follow us? Then we'll explain everything."

VEILED THREATS

The two men led Hiram and the others out of that chamber through a gap in the walls they hadn't seen before. It was either impossible to see because of the dark, or — and Hiram thought this was getting into Hollywood territory — or there was some kind of sliding, magical door like something out of The Temple of Doom. Either way, it was beyond him right now. Then again, this whole thing was beyond Hiram's imagination. They'd set out for a bit of fun after hearing a story that, quite frankly, he hadn't really bought into. It had just sounded more fun than sitting around in pubs for a few days, though there was certainly nothing wrong with that.

After chatting with Ian the vicar in Saint Giles church back in Nottingham, and learning the Stone Man statue pointed to the secret caves, and then making their way to those caves, only to find mysterious carvings and symbology, and some evocative words etched into the stone that seemed to point south... Well, things had really escalated. At ancient Avebury they'd found more enigmatic carvings. Then his car had been destroyed. Then they'd discovered a secret entrance into Europe's largest burial mound, only to be attacked by apparent assassins from foreign shores. If that wasn't all bizarre enough, they'd just been assisted by... Templars? Really? You couldn't make this shit up.

The next chamber was vast, and was unlike anything any of them had ever seen before. Hiram figured they must almost be in the very centre of the mound, and somewhere towards the top. The angled walls formed a five-sided pentagon, above which was a high vaulted ceiling. The walls and ceiling were carved with dozens, maybe hundreds of stylised symbols that referenced the Templar's history, the Crusades, Christianity and other familiar images associated with the Knights Templar.

Alongside those images were others Hiram wouldn't have expected to see; symbols more associated with Islam, Judaism, even Hinduism and Buddhism.

"Not what you were expecting, was it," said the man who'd called himself James. The words were more statement than question.

"No. Nothing at all like... like I expected. To be fair, I didn't expect any of this." The first hint of a smile found its way into Hiram's eyes. He stepped closer to one of the walls. "Those are all symbols of monotheist religions. Why? I thought Temp —"

"... thought Templars were Christian? We are. Always have been, and we always will be. Christianity was our faith back in the time of the Crusades, and why we even existed in the first place. But history has a funny way of distorting the facts, ignoring truths, disregarding reality and, in some cases, covering up terrible, heinous and catastrophic mistakes. I digress. Forgive me. Tell me though, why is it you're really here? I mean, I think I know. But why don't you make sure I've read this situation correctly."

Hiram glanced first at Alex, then at Evan. Their faces displayed pure bewilderment, and he felt sure they were mirrors of his own. Because he was very, very bewildered. He turned back to the men. "We were drinking at Ye Olde Trip to Jerusalem, a pub in Nottingham... just below the castle. Do you know it?"

James and John shared a look, then smiled ruefully. "Sorry. Yes, we know it. Please, go on."

"We were having a few pints when we met an old man who called himself Steven Stalbridge." Hiram paused to gauge their reaction, and immediately sensed they knew who Steven was. "We got chatting, and he told us a story about how he believed he was related to the last known Templar knight in

England. He seemed both sad and excited about it. He told us that if we wanted an adventure, perhaps we'd go off and find the truth."

John nodded. "And where did this... this adventure? Where did it start?" he asked. John seemed the slightly younger of the two men, though they looked very much alike and it was clear they were brothers.

"The Stone Man," said Evan, joining in and no longer fearing for his life. "Steven said to search out the Stone Man."

"And did you find it? My guess is yes."

"We did. We also spoke with a vicar, Ian. He explained a little about the origin of the Stone Man... Tommy? Then directed us towards a secret cave complex in Shropshire... though I don't think it's very secret anymore."

"Caynton Caves," James declared. "No, not exactly secret any more," he added, though there was no malice evident in his words.

"What about the two men who attacked you? Do you know who they were?" John asked.

"No, we don't," Hiram answered. "We uh, we were hoping you might tell us."

The brothers remained silent for a while, as if deciding how much to tell Hiram and his friends. After a moment, James nodded to his brother. John turned to Hiram.

"What's your name? You look somehow familiar to me."

"Me?" John nodded. "My name's Hiram. Hiram Kane. I'm a Master's student at the University of East Anglia in Norwich. My grandfather is Hiram Kane Snr. He's on the board of trustees at the British Museum. My great-grandfather was —"

"... Patrick Kane... the man who rediscovered Machu Picchu with Hiram Bingham?"

"Uh, yes. That's right. How did you —"

"In our world," James said, "it's important to keep a track of people who, shall we say, might have an interest in learning our secret? Your name has been on our radar for several years, along with other history and religious scholars, archaeologists... treasure hunters." He grinned, and for the first time Hiram and the others relaxed... if only a little. "Don't worry though," James continued, "our order has never considered you or your family a threat. In fact, quite the opposite."

"Indeed," John added. "We've always known that one day someone would work out the clues and find us here. We just didn't think it would take almost seven-hundred years."

"You mean we're the first?" Hiram asked, incredulous.

"Not exactly. Many of our enemies have found us. None have ever made it as far as you. And none ever return. But you, Hiram, and your friends... you're the first group to have found us who didn't mean to cause us harm. For that we consider ourselves very fortunate." He glanced at his brother, who nodded. "Now there's something serious to discuss. It's something our order has been doing its best to keep a secret since Friday, October the thirteenth, 1307. I'm confident we'll come to a very acceptable agreement," James added, his face now deadly serious. "In fact, you have no choice."

THREE VOWS, ONE OATH

James' last words carried just the trace of a threat, though Hiram sensed it was more precautionary than real.

If they really were the first people to have ever been here who weren't considered the enemy, then whatever secrets they kept here were obviously serious. Hiram's family had a long history of exploration, stretching right back to Patrick Kane and Machu Picchu. Their reputation as philanthropists and sensitive archaeologists was well-deserved. Hiram had no desire to tarnish that reputation now.

"So who were those men?" he asked. "I mean, I guess we're responsible for them coming here. They obviously followed us. Um, sorry about that."

"Don't be sorry," John said. "It's a compliment to you and your friends that they did follow you. They wouldn't have found us otherwise. As to who they were, I shall try and explain. But first you must all swear that whatever you hear in this chamber today remains between the three of you and never leaves these walls. You'll understand why once you know. And, I happen to believe we're safe to tell you. Do you swear to keep your silence?"

Hiram looked at Alex and Evan, whose eyes were forced wide in amazement by the whole experience. But he knew them, knew their characters. This, Hiram had zero doubt at all about their ability and desire to do the right thing, whatever the circumstances. They both nodded. Hiram turned back to the brothers. "On behalf of myself and my friends, I swear that whatever we learn here today shall never be discussed by any of us again. You have our word. You have my word."

"And your word, Hiram Kane, is good enough for us."

"Let me show you something," John said as he stepped over to a shelf carved directly into the stone wall. He gathered up a small object, then returned to his position in front of Hiram and the others. He opened his hands to reveal a golden object the size of a Digestive biscuit. It looked like some kind of medal. On its surface was carved the same goat-headed icon they'd seen carved into the bedrock at Caynton Caves, on the stone at Avebury, and on the walls within the chamber here at Silbury Hill. "Do you know what this is and what it represents?"

"I think it's Baphomet," Alex said. "Usually considered to be a sign of devil worship, but actually more often used as just the opposite."

"Very good, um...?"

"Alex. Alexandria Ridley."

"Very good Alex," John said. "And do you know the origin of the word Baphomet?" She didn't. "Many scholars believe, as do we, the word Baphomet is simply the result of many generations of mistranslation, perhaps misinterpretation, of another word from that part of the world. Think about all those differing tribes and cultures and voices, and how the word Mohammed might end up being translated."

"Mohammed? You mean, Baphomet is really just a garbled version of Mohammed?" Alex was shocked.

"That's what we believe, yes."

"So by continuing to apply representations of Baphomet in Templar iconography, they, and now you, are really displaying an affinity for the Islamic prophet Mohammed? Is that what you mean?"

"Precisely. And can you guess where this beautiful artefact came from?"

No one answered, so John continued. "Somewhere near the end of the thirteenth-century, one of our ancestors was into his third Crusade in the Holy Land. Now, most people believe the Crusades were a simple case of Christians versus Muslims in a fight for control over the Holy Lands, in what is now the

Middle-East. And that is almost correct. However, there is more to it than that. A lot more. What the history books don't tell us is that many factions of the Crusaders actually admired some of the customs the so-called enemy adhered to. Of course, in those days that enemy was Islam. The truth is, Islam is essentially a peaceful religion. Now, I'm not going to get into a philosophical discussion about the rights or wrongs of this religion or that religion. I think we can agree that all organised religions these days are flawed in one way or another. I'm not even going to discuss whether my brother and I are even true Christians any more, despite the fact we are very clearly still representing the Templars and, by default, Christianity."

James' face took on an enigmatic expression, as if he knew what he'd said would come as a great surprise to Hiram and the others. In that he was right.

Hiram wondered aloud. "If you aren't true Christians, why are you still defending whatever this secret is from your so-called enemies? And this place? Is it some kind of Templar bastion?"

The brothers shared a glance. Both grinned. "Good questions," James said. "But let me continue. As for this artefact, it was given to my ancestor by someone he was trying to kill. They were on a battlefield in Acre, north of Jerusalem. My ancestor and his adversary, a Mamluk warrior named Mahmud, were locked in fierce hand-to-hand contact. They had both suffered serious injuries and were each as exhausted as the other. After many minutes of fighting, both men slumped to the ground, almost unable to continue the fight. They each sat there, resting back on their arms and staring at each other, afraid they were being tricked.

"There was nobody else around. Both had been separated from their men. Finally, the Mamluk warrior said something to our ancestor. In English, he said 'Sorry'. The story goes that he reached into his armour and pulled something out. Then he stood up and took a few steps towards our ancestor, leaving his weapons on the ground behind him. Too tired to even stand, our ancestor was powerless now to do anything even if he was attacked. Instead of attacking though, the Mamluk came closer and sat down on the ground in front of him. Extending his hand, he passed over this golden medal."

John handed the artefact to Hiram, who took it gently and held it closer for Alex and Evan to see. It was a beautiful object, and glowed beneath the light of the flaming torches. It reminded him of his own Inca sun disc, given to him by his grandfather a decade before and which in that very moment was hanging on a strap around his neck

"It's lovely," Alex said.

"Very cool indeed," agreed Evan.

"What's the big secret though?" Hiram asked, eager to learn more. "And why is it so important?"

"Okay, now to the real question," James said.

"In many ways Islam is like Christianity. Of course, their histories share many of the same historical characters and philosophies as ours. One of the most obvious things they shared traditionally was that it was forbidden to worship idols. Now, in today's world idolatry is largely ignored in Christianity... most people have a crucifix hanging somewhere in their home, for example. However, in Islam it is still a cardinal sin. It's known in Arabic as a *shirk*, the sin of idolatry. That is a direct and heinous contradiction of the virtue of *Tawhid*, or in English, monotheism. It remains a sin punishable by death..."

Hiram and his the others listened carefully to James' words. It made sense. But none of them saw what this had to do with anything now. "I'm sorry, James," Hiram said, "but I fail to see what the problem is. Who is worshipping false idols, and why does it matter?"

"Okay, fair point. Did you get a good look at those guys who followed you?"

"No, not really. Why? Who were they?"

"They're from a rogue band of Islamic fundamentalists... with a difference. These two men were not terrorists, not exactly. Their main aim, their personal Jihad, if you like, is to help undermine Christianity by revealing the truth; that is, that after the Crusades many Christians actually worshipped very non-Christian entities."

"Like Baphomet?" Alex asked.

"Yes. Like Baphomet." James offered a smiled.

"But what would that do? What would it prove?" Hiram still didn't get it.

"Think about it. In this world of growing religious tensions and escalating friction between Christianity and Islam, the powers-that-be in Christianity do not want it to become widespread knowledge that for centuries many of their flock were actually following some of the Islamic codes. Conversely, as I just mentioned, in Islam the very act of worshipping false idols is a mortal sin punishable by death. The only thing worse than a Muslim doing that is —"

"... is a Christian doing it." Hiram thought he'd finally understood it. "And, if Islamic fundamentalists needed any more motivation to carry out their Jihadist attacks against infidels, exposing the fact that descendants of the mightiest of the Crusaders, the Templar Knights, still exist, and further more, are still worshipping Islamic icons, then —"

"... then let's just say," John cut in, "that the world does not need to suffer the consequences of that. Not now, not ever."

"Which is why we're still here," James continued, "and still defending our last stronghold.

"Still fighting to keep our secret," added John

Hiram nodded. It was all becoming clear.

Dramatic, for sure. But then again, if there was even the slightest chance that if these men were discovered, and the truth got out about how for centuries Christians had been defiling Islamic icons, it would be inviting an act of revenge so great it could conceivably result in a new World War.

THE ANCESTOR

"So there you have it," James said. "Now you know who we are and why we're here."

"That's not exactly true," Evan said. He'd been very quiet until now. For Hiram that had been as shocking as anything else today. "You've told us your names, but that's about it."

"Fair point," John agreed. "Well as you know I'm John and this is my older brother James. You remember we told you about the Templar Knight who was given that gold artefact Hiram's holding? His name was James too. James de Somervila. He was the leader of the last known band of Templar Knights who fled for their lives after the accusations of heresy. I say accusations. The fact is, the accusations were in some way true. What wasn't true was their alleged disloyalty to the Pope and the King of

England. That should never have been questioned. It was true that those Knights and many like them admired some of the customs they'd picked up in the Holy Lands. But it all started when the Mamluk warrior Mamhud gave that one knight that very medal you're holding."

"James de Somervila," Hiram said.

"James de Somervila. Our ancestor."

"Wait. Does that mean you're literally the last Templar Knights in England?" Evan asked.

"Ha, you think we're Knights?" James said, more than a little amused.

"We saw how you took down that man so easily out there," Alex said.

"Well I admit, we have some combat skills. But so does Hiram." Again, he tipped his head at Hiram, respect evident in his eyes. "But Knights? That's preposterous." John bellowed in laughter, and it was a joyful sound.

"Not Knights," James said. "But the last descendants of the Templars in England? Well yes, we believe that's true. Thus, the mantle has fallen upon us to retain our secret... our grail, if you will. That is, until we're gone and our children take over."

"Speak for yourself, old timer," John said. "I'm living another hundred years."

The atmosphere now was light-hearted. But there still remained the serious issue of the two

Muslim men detained somewhere within the depths of Silbury Hill.

Evan couldn't help himself. "What about those men? The ones who followed us here? What will happen to them?"

A moment of silence passed, before James finally spoke. "Look, I think you'll agree that what we do here is vitally important for many reasons, not least in us doing our part for world peace. I know that sounds dramatic, and it probably is. But we really believe it's that important and we can't take any risks." He paused, fixing his eyes on Evan. "It is better if you don't ask any further questions about that. Let's just say we are confident our secret will remain hidden beneath this ancient hill."

James' eyes flicked from Evan's to Alex's, and finally Hiram's. He held their gazes, almost challenging them to question his words. None of them did.

"But I'll say this. You have my word they will not be harmed. Is that good enough?"

Hiram and the others saw only honesty in James' eyes. And, just like Hiram's word had been enough for James, James' word was enough for them.

"If it's okay I have a different question," Alex said, changing the subject. "We saw the word prōditōr carved into the cave wall at Caynton. Traitor, or the betrayer. Can you tell us who the traitor was?"

James and John shared another look. After a moment, John took a deep breath, then said, "Yes, we can tell you. I don't think you'll like what you hear. Besides, your adventure isn't over just yet, and there's someone far more equipped to help you understand that part of the story."

NOTHING TO SEE HERE

"So do we have an agreement, Hiram?" James asked.

"Yes, sir, we do. You have my word that after today we will never speak of this again. I promise."

James looked for a long moment into Hiram's brownish green eyes. He saw in them an intensity, an intensity matched in equal parts by both integrity and honesty. James was certain they could trust Hiram to keep his word.

"Then may we bid you farewell," James said. "We wish you a safe journey, and may all your adventures be fruitful."

"There's just one more thing to say before you leave," John added. "Stow Longa."

"Stow what?" Evan asked. "What's a Stow Longie?"

"Stow Longa," John repeated. "Find yourselves a map."

With that, Hiram, Alex and Evan were ushered back into the chamber from which they'd first ascended into the depths of Silbury Hill, and sent on their way after what was the most unbelievable hour of any of their lives.

"Did that even just happen?" Alex muttered, her head shaking in disbelief. "I mean, was I dreaming?"

"I know. I can't believe what we've just witnessed," Hiram agreed.

They emerged from the small entrance to the chamber into a crisp, clear day with not a snow cloud anywhere in sight.

"Well, it definitely happened," Evan added. "I've got the bruises to prove it. Smashed my shoulder on the stone wall when I dived for cover when those... the two men were about to attack us."

"You okay?" Hiram asked.

"Yeah, fine." Evan fell silent for a second. "What do you think they'll do to them? I mean, the two men. Will they kill them?"

"Honestly mate, I don't know. I want to think the answer is no," Hiram said. He didn't believe the descendants of the Templars would kill the two Muslim men. The brothers didn't seem to be murderers. Then again, Hiram wondered if some things might just be worth killing for. Ironically, world peace might be one of them. He had never thought about it that way before. He'd always hated injustices, hated anything that hurt someone who didn't deserve it. But this was bigger than him. Bigger than any of them. How could he know what was the right thing to do, when something as enormous as world peace was potentially at stake? In the end he decided that he was unequipped at this stage in his life to know how far someone should go to protect the truth, especially with so much at stake.

"Let's just assume that those men, James and John, know what they're doing. Okay?"

Evan nodded. He didn't like not knowing what would become of the men. Despite the fact they might very well have killed him if the Templars hadn't stepped in, he didn't like the thought of them being killed in return. Two wrongs didn't always make a right. He shook his head and tried to put it out of his mind.

"There's Luke," Alex said as they climbed the steps up from the grassy pasture surrounding Silbury Hill and into the car park, "sitting in that ugly brown car. Is that... that's not a Fiat Uno, is it?"

"Good lad," Hiram said. "I mean, good lad for finding a hire car, not for his choice."

"Alright guys," called Luke as he climbed out of the monstrosity of a car he'd hired in Marlborough. "Did you find a way inside?" he asked. "What was it like?"

Hiram glanced at Evan, then at Alex. They both nodded subtly back.

"Nothing, mate," Hiram answered. "Nothing at all. Complete waste of time."

CROSS THE PAGE

"Has this delightfully cosy car got a map in the glove box?" Hiram asked, mocking Luke's choice of vehicle.

"Don't know. Let me look." He pulled down the glove box lid and pulled out a road atlas. "Yep. Where're we going?"

"Stow Longa," Hiram said. "Ever heard of it?"

"Don't think so. What's there?"

"The truth about a traitor," Alex said. "Let's go... if this thing makes it that far."

"What's wrong with it?" Luke asked.

"Didn't they have anything, um, adult sized?" Evan said. "Smallest damn car on the road. And brown?"

"Perfect for your little legs, eh?" Alex teased. Evan couldn't argue with that.

They found Stow Longa on the map. It was approximately a three and a half hour drive, so they set off, not before stopping back for supplies in the small market town of Marlborough.

"Didn't they have any better choices?" Evan persisted as they stepped out. "A Skoda would've been better than this."

Hiram steered them out of town and onto the M4. The banter about the car had ceased and they'd fallen into silence, each of them trying to come to terms with the morning's events. Of course, Luke didn't know all that had transpired since they'd left him at Avebury. He couldn't know, and they would never tell him. Hiram figured it was why Evan had been so enthusiastic in teasing Luke about the car... because he wanted to deflect from thinking about what had happened. He didn't blame him. They'd made a promise not to talk about what they'd seen and who they'd discovered in the depths of Silbury Hill, and he trusted each of the others to keep that secret.

Whether he should keep it or not though was troubling Hiram. The brothers had seemed genuine and legitimate. And yet, he only had their word to go on. What if he was wrong? What if they were the bad guys and the other two men were trying to do something good? At this stage, after all that had happened, Hiram didn't know. Maybe they'd learn more at Stow Longa, wherever the hell that was. He had no idea what they'd find there. But if it wasn't something, or someone, that would back up what they'd been told down at Silbury Hill, he'd have to give some serious thought about going to the authorities and reporting the abduction of the two men.

It was a little after three when Hiram left the A1 dual carriageway in Cambridgeshire and veered towards the tiny remote hamlet of Stow Longa. The sky had stayed mercifully clear for the drive north but the sun was sinking lower and he figured they had just a few hour's more daylight left at most.

They entered the small village with little or no expectations of what to expect, and had driven only several hundred yards when the road opened up and a small village green appeared on their left. Slap bang in the middle of that green was something that made Hiram pull the car to a sharp stop.

"Reckon that's out next clue, don't you?" he said.

"Must be," Alex agreed.

"Um, sorry for my ignorance," Luke said, "but a clue for what? Why the hell are we here? And how did you know about this place?"

This is going to be awkward. "Listen, mate," Hiram said, "you'll just have to trust us, okay? I can't tell you any more than that. Whatever we might find up here in Stow Longa is fair game, but we can't tell you any more about what's already happened and what we learned down south. Sorry."

Luke nodded. He had known Hiram a few

years now, and knew him to be as honest, ethical and principled as anyone he'd ever known. "I understand. I can't say I'm not disappointed, but I get it."

Hiram nodded. He'd feel the same if the shoe was on the other foot. "Right, let's check this out."

They piled out of the car, huddling into their jackets as the winter cold bit into their exposed skin.

"Well, what do you know," Evan said, striding up to the small stone monument in the middle of the green. "I'd bet my life savings this was once a Templar cross."

"My friend," Hiram said calmly, "your life savings wouldn't even fill that car with petrol. But I agree... could be Templar."

"How do we know for sure?" Luke asked. "The top's missing, isn't it?"

"Yes, Luke's right," Alex agreed. The stone pillar, sitting on an ornate hexagonal stone plinth, finished abruptly about four-feet high. The top was smooth, as if designed that way. But Alex guessed that it had just been worn smooth by either decades and decades of harsh weather, or destroyed by some anti-Templar iconoclasts centuries ago. Alex stepped closer, searching for more of the carved Templar icons. She was joined by the others, but after a brief search revealed no sign of Templar symbology, they wondered if they were wrong about it after all. Either way, without seeing the top half of the stone pillar that might once have been a Templar cross, they couldn't be sure.

Then Alex spotted a church tower sticking up above the row of houses surrounding the quintessential English green. "Why don't we check the church," she suggested. "Maybe we'll have some luck there."

They hustled back into the car and Hiram drove them around the green and up the adjoining road. Moments later they were entering the church. The sun was sinking rapidly to the west and the day's light was dwindling away.

"I've been expecting you."

The voice startled them all. They spun around to see a rather rotund middle-aged woman standing there, a warm smile spreading across her rosy cheeks. "Oh, forgive me, I didn't mean to scare you. Please accept my apologies."

"That's okay," Hiram said. "I guess we're a little on edge."

"Understandable," said the woman. "My name's Mary."

Alex stepped forward and shook the woman's hand. "Hello Mary. I'm Alex. You said you were expecting us?"

"Yes, I was. Let's just say a friend of mine... of ours... called and said to expect visitors later today. And here you are." The smile grew even wider, and there seemed nothing but genuine kindness in it.

Hiram stepped forward too. "My name's Hiram, and these are our friends, Evan and Luke. It's nice to meet you."

They exchanged pleasantries. Then Hiram turned serious. "Mary, maybe you can help us?"

"I will most certainly try," Mary said, "and I believe I can."

"There's a stone plinth in the village green. We think that it's... was... a Templar cross. I suspect you can confirm that's true?"

"Yes, my dear. I can confirm that's true. Would you like me to prove it?"

With a slightly waddling stride, Mary led them to the rear of the church and through a door. Then, after pulling on a thick coat, she opened an external door and led them out into the graveyard, sunset still an hour and a half away, despite the gloom. She turned back to face the church and opened her arms out, as if to show them something. "There," she said.

Hiram and the others turned. There against the wall was the other half of the Templar cross, now set onto a new pedestal and glimmering under the fading winter light. Hiram nodded. "I also wanted to ask you about —"

"Perhaps you should take a look at that." Mary pointed to a covered lychgate at the western edge of the cemetery, though from their position Hiram and the others couldn't see anything other than the standard covered churchyard entrance. "Go on, go and take a look."

Hiram led the others along the gravel path, swung open the gates beneath the thatched arch and stepped through onto the path. He couldn't help but smile. There beside the gateway, standing tall and apparently proud, and with his right arm raised and pointing west, his other clutching a sword by his side, was another Stone Man. This one however was completely undamaged.

"Wow," Hiram said, eloquent as ever.

"He's beautiful," Alex said.

"I'm hungry," added Evan.

"You're always hungry," confirmed Luke.

"Mary, that's west isn't it?" Alex asked.

"Actually my dear," Mary said, "slightly north west. If you look between those two houses over there, where the sun's angling, that's west. If you go now, I think you'll just about make it before dark."

"Make it where?" Hiram asked. He had no idea where 'where' was.

"Follow me," Mary said, and they duly did. Their excitement was rising. They were closing in on something, and they all felt it.

Once they were back inside the church Mary led them to a small table in the corner. From her purse she pulled a notebook and a pen. A moment later she had sketched an accurate outlined map of Britain.

"Okay," she said. "I've been informed you started your journey in Nottingham, is that correct?"

Hiram nodded, and Mary marked the map with a dot roughly where the city of Nottingham would be. She handed the pen to Hiram. "Okay, where did you go next?"

"Uh, Caynton. In Shropshire."

Mary nodded and looked at Hiram, a knowing look in her eyes. "Go ahead, mark it on the map."

Hiram looked at the sketch and touched the pen down where he thought Caynton would be. "Here?" he asked.

"Up just a tiny bit," Alex said.

"Yes, just a little bit north," Luke agreed. Hiram marked the drawing with another dot.

"And where next?" Mary asked.

"Avebury," Hiram said.

Evan leaned in and placed his fingertip on the map. "Right there," he said, "right?"

"Yep," Alex agreed. Hiram marked the spot again.

"And where are we now?"

"Stow Longa," Hiram said, "about... here?" He touched the tip of the pen down again.

Mary gently shifted his hand down the map a centimetre. "Right there," she said, and Hiram duly marked the map. "And? Do you see anything?"

"Well, I see a lovely little sketch of Britain with some equally lovely dots on it. Other than that..."

Alex stared hard at the map, tilting her head a little, as if seeing something but not quite understanding what. Then, she said, "Got it." She took the pen from Hiram and carefully drew a straight line, starting at Nottingham and connecting that dot with the dot that represented Avebury, or more accurately, Silbury Hill. Next she touched the pen down on Stow Longa and, very slowly, drew a straight line across the map. That line connected Stow Longa in the east with Caynton in the west.

"Voila!"

The others looked on in amazement. The visual representation made it clear.

It was a perfect cross. Hiram looked down at the map, the grin on his face masking his disappointment at not working it all out sooner himself.

They'd been on a circuitous route of the country, and each stop they'd made had marked the cardinal points of a cross.

"And would you care to take a guess at where the very centre of this great nation lies?" Mary asked.

Alex looked at Hiram. His expression told her, *go ahead. So,* she leaned in and marked a large dot on the spot where the two lines of the cross intersected.

"Bingo," declared Mary.

"What's there?" Alex asked. "Is it a town?"

"No, much smaller than a town." Mary took the pen from Alex and scrawled a couple of words on the left of the page.

Fenny Drayton

"Fenny Drayton?" Luke asked.

"Yes, Fenny Drayton, the beating heart of this country. And wouldn't you just know it... that's exactly the direction our friend at the gate is pointing."

"And does your friend at the gate have a name?" Evan asked. "I mean, we've already met Tommy Templar up in Nottingham..."

"I'm afraid not. Our statue is just a plain old Templar statue. My brother Ian was always the childish one." Mary winked, and led the friends out of the church. "Like I said, go now, and find the heart of our country."

"But what'll we find there?" Hiram asked.

"Oh, I don't know," Mary said. "Let's just assume you're going to see a man about a goat."

A MAN ABOUT A GOAT

"A man about a goat, huh?" Evan said as Hiram sped them out of Stow Longa and angled slightly north west toward Fenny Drayton.

Despite Mary's somewhat cryptic words, Hiram felt sure they would be glad they made this last leg of the journey. Why? He wasn't sure. But they had come so far in just two long days. It was only an hour or so to the final dot on their map, and there was no reason not to go the proverbial extra mile.

"That's what she said," Hiram answered, "a man about a goat, though isn't the expression usually 'see a man about a horse?'"

"It is," agreed Alex. "I guess with yet another reference to goats, meaning Baphomet, I suppose we're still on some kind of grail trail."

"Grail trail? I like it," Hiram said, chuckling.

"Seems that way," Luke said.

"I'm still hungry," Evan added. "You think there'll be food at this Fenny Drayton place? Goat kebab?"

"Eww, disgusting," said Alex. "Can't think of anything worse."

"Looking at the map," Luke said," it seems to me there's no significant village or town anywhere near this place."

Evan grumbled something about *wasting away* as Hiram edged off the A14 and onto the wider A5. "Not long now, maybe twenty minutes. Might just make it before sunset."

Fifteen minutes later they saw the first signpost for Fenny Drayton. Hiram veered off the highway onto what was a narrow, undulating country road. He followed that for five miles before it ended at a small village. It was almost dark now and he switched on the tiny Fiat's headlights. "Okay, where now?"

"There," Alex said. "You see it? That sign says Drayton's Goat Sanctuary. Must be it."

Hiram agreed, and drove past the sign and down a long, winding lane. The small car felt every bone-jarring lump and bump keenly as it jostled them towards what was apparently a goat sanctuary over the unfinished trail. Five minutes later, they came to a fence. A large sign declared:

Drayton's Goat Sanctuary

Sorry, We're Closed

"Oh great," Evan whined. "All this way and it's —"

Just then the double large gates swung slowly open. Behind them stood another of the oldest men Hiram had ever seen, older even than Steven Stalbridge back at Ye Olde Trip to Jerusalem. The beam of the Fiat's headlights illuminated the man's long white beard, a beard that hung down to his considerable chest. Despite his large coat they saw it concealed an impressive physique beneath. On his head sat a wide straw hat. The old man wore a pair of tall wellington boots, complete with mud.

Smiling, he waved them through the gates and Hiram drove through. Once they were inside, the gates automatically swung closed behind them. In the near darkness, in such a remote place, and with the gates now closed behind them, they should have felt leery of the situation. Yet none of them did. It was just another odd situation in a series of very odd situations.

"Welcome to Drayton's," the man said as they climbed out of the car, his voice deep and sonorous. "I'm Fenny. I understand you've come to see a man about a goat."

Hiram chuckled, then introduced himself and his friends.

"Pleasure to meet you too, Hiram. All of you."

"Look, Fenny... it's just that we don't know why we're here. I'm sure it's not to see any goats."

Fenny laughed, and it was the laugh of someone completely at ease with the world. "I imagine this is all a little confusing for you. You may have worked out by now that we have friends all around the country. A network of like-minded people who all play a vital role in what we do. As I believe you now know, that is to keep an important secret. Please, come this way."

Fenny led them away from the small gravel car park. They passed a couple of large farm-type buildings on their left and some open paddocks to their right.

"Is this really a goat sanctuary?" asked Alex. It kind of looked like a farm, but, as a lifelong vegetarian she didn't like the idea of animals being bred for food.

"Yes, my dear, it really is. This used to be a farm back in the day, but when the chance came to buy it, oh, way back in the sixties, our organisation took it over. We shut down the farming operation and turned it into a sanctuary for abandoned farm animals. Of course, that's not all we do. But it's a cause we're passionate about. It's a very useful cover, don't you think?"

"Yes, definitely a great cause," Alex agreed.

Darkness had almost consumed the sanctuary

and the surrounding countryside, despite it being only four thirty in the afternoon. All the rescued animals were safely tucked into their warm barns for the night and out of the bitter cold. The winter solstice was two days ago, and Hiram longed for spring to hurry up and bring the longer, warmer days with it.

Fenny led them over to an ancient stone outhouse, probably no more than a dozen foot across and twenty feet long. It was topped by a low thatched roof that looked as if it needed replacing sooner rather than later. "Please, come inside," Fenny said, unlocking the door with a large key.

They stepped inside and Fenny switched on a few overhead lights. Inside was a kind of barn, nondescript in appearance and with a few chairs and tables dotted around. The first thing they all noticed, however, was how warm it was. Hiram had expected it to be cold, based on the state of the roof. He glanced up. What he saw surprised him. Instead of a thatched roof full of gaping holes letting in the wintry elements, he saw a nicely finished ceiling, with both heaters and air-conditioning units dotted around.

"Those are a bit fancy for an old stone barn, aren't they?" he asked.

"Aye, you're right," Fenny replied. "Bit fancy for an old barn." He winked, and Hiram saw a definite trace of mischief in his eyes. "Why don't I make us a pot of tea," he said, and walked over to a small kitchenette at the far side of the barn. "Go on, grab a seat."

Hiram and the others took a seat at the central table, looks of uncertainty passing between them. They just couldn't see what they might possibly learn out here in the middle of nowhere. A couple of minutes later Fenny returned with a tray laden with tea cups, a large pot of tea and, to Evan's delight, a well-stocked biscuit barrel.

"I know why you're here," Fenny said. "You met a man in a pub who told you an evocative story. That man suggested you might help him find out the truth about his ancestors. Is that accurate?" he asked, though it wasn't a question.

"That's exactly it," Hiram answered. "We've had a hell of an adventure, and as you know we've learned some things we probably weren't ever meant to learn." Fenny nodded, and Hiram continued. "As yet, we haven't learned the one thing we set out to learn. So please, Fenny, tell us about Steven Stalbridge?"

Fenny Drayton nodded. He'd been expecting the question. "I promise we'll get to that shortly. First, let me show you something that might add a little more credence to our story here."

Fenny led them over to a darkened red-brick fireplace in the centre of the rear wall. The fire remained unlit. Upon closer inspection, Hiram realised it was actually a kind of altar, yet it was an altar unlike any he had ever seen before. Dotted around the large hearth were examples of Christian iconography; crosses, both Templar and otherwise, a golden chalice, and a mixture of other items. Alongside those, however, were representations from all the other religions, including Islam, Judaism, Catholicism, Hindu, Jainism, Buddhism and many other, lesser known religions from around the world. There were also atheist symbols, and next to those, sketches of Charles Darwin, Albert Einstein and other notable historical thinkers from a vast field of disciplines.

Hiram didn't know what to say. Neither did the others. Hiram was not a religious man in any way, and while respecting the beliefs of others he'd always considered organised religion to be a negative influence on society, despite some of the good those organisations did. Finally, he managed, "What is this, Fenny? I mean, I can see it's an altar, but an altar to... to everything?"

"Yes, in a way, it is. This altar is meant to be a visual manifestation of what our order now believes. That is, that all religions are as good as each other, and also as bad. Practiced and taught in the right manner, religion is harmless. But in the wrong minds and in the wrong hands..."

Hiram nodded. He noticed his friends were also in agreement.

"Listen," Fenny continued, "I know some of what's going on was explained to you by my brothers down in Wiltshire. By now you've probably guessed we're all descendants of the Templars in some way. And yes, the two men you met at Silbury Hill are my sons. Ian, the vicar at St Giles is my nephew. Mary in Stow Longa is my niece, Ian's sister. There are less than a hundred of us now, all dotted around the country in strategic places that, for hundreds of years, curious folks like yourselves, and other more nefarious types, have gone searching for answers. Unfortunately, not all of those people are as nice and genuine as you youngsters. There are others out there, unscrupulous people whose philosophy still clings onto a belief system from the middle ages, and who, if they were ever to reveal what we're hiding, well... The consequences don't bear thinking about. Thus, we firmly believe our secret is a secret worth protecting. Worth protecting at any cost. The question is, are you in agreement?"

"Fenny, we already swore to keep or silence to your sons, James and John. They asked us the same questions, and we swore to them we would never utter a word about what we saw at Silbury Hill to anyone. And we won't. I promise, Fenny, none of us here will ever mention any of this again." He glanced at Luke. "Not even to each other."

Fenny Drayton let his pale eyes linger on Hiram's for long seconds. He had already been told about Hiram's declaration in a phone call with his son James, and he'd believed it. He just needed to hear the words for himself. And now that he had, he was as convinced as his sons had been that Hiram was an honourable and ethical man.

"Well, I'll tell you know that I don't doubt you, Hiram, nor do I doubt your friends. Listen," he said, "it's Christmas Eve, and forgive me if I'm wrong, but shouldn't kids like you be out drinking in a pub on Christmas Eve?"

"Yes, and we should be eating in a pub too," Evan said.

"It's almost six o'clock. My wife will be expecting me over at the house for dinner soon. Would you do me the honour of joining my wife and I for dinner and a Christmas drink while I tell you what you really wanted to know when you set out on this journey? It's just over yonder in the main farmhouse. Then, you can head back to Nottingham and be in the pub by eight o'clock —"

"We accept," Evan said almost before Fenny had finished his sentence.

Ten minutes later, Hiram, Alex, Evan and Luke were sitting around Gwen Drayton's dining table. A fire roared in the hearth and, for the first time in what felt like days, they finally warmed up.

"Thanks for the drinks, Mrs Drayton," Alex said, sipping her glass of wine.

"Please, it's Gwen. The only person who calls me

Mrs Drayton is Fenny, and only when he's done something wrong." Gwen disappeared out into the kitchen and left Fenny with Hiram and the others.

"So," Hiram said, "I think you were going to tell us about old Steven Stalbridge?"

SILENT KNIGHTS

"Stalbridge sounds like olde-world English, doesn't it?" asked Fenny. "Middle ages even?"

"Yes, I suppose it does," Alex agreed.

"And you'd be right, relatively speaking. But I'm sure you know that names, and their pronunciations, change over the course of time. Anyway, Stalbridge is the name of a family that hailed from Yorkshire hundreds of years ago, and who were Lords of the Manor of Starbeck, near Harrogate. But you should also be aware of this... the Stalbridges were the descendants of the —"

"... the Stapelbriggs," Hiram finished. He had suddenly put the pieces together, and it wasn't looking good for Steven. "Our old friend in the pub wasn't a descendant of the heroic so-called Last Templar after all. His ancestor was the traitor, Stephen de Stapelbrigg."

Fenny Drayton nodded, a hint of sadness in his eyes. "I'm sorry that wasn't the 'truth' you sought on this adventure. I really am."

"Not as sorry as Steven's going to be," Alex said.

"Poor old fella's going to be devastated," added Luke. "He's been searching years, decades even, to learn the truth about his famed ancestor. He'll be crushed to learn that it was *his* ancestor who betrayed the last Templars and caused them to run for their lives."

Hiram and the others thanked Gwen and Fenny Drayton for their hospitality and for the delicious meal. It was seven thirty, and with an hour or so drive to get back to Nottingham, they wasted no time. With full bellies and beer on their minds — especially Hiram, who'd abstained at dinner due to being the driver — they left. Not before asking one more question of Fenny.

"Sorry Fenny, but I have one further question," Hiram said.

"Of course, son, ask me anything. Well, almost anything."

"This sanctuary... a goat sanctuary. Is that a kind of coded reference to, uh, Baphomet?"

Fenny glanced at his wife, Gwen, whose face remained stoic, other than an almost imperceptible curving of her lips. Fenny turned back to Hiram, his own face passive but the hint of amusement crinkling his eyes. He ran a hand down the length of his long white beard, then looked deep into Hiram's eyes. With an almost straight face, he said, "No son, it isn't. We just really like goats." The wink that followed told Hiram and the others all they needed to know.

Fenny and Gwen watched as Hiram steered the car through the open gates and watched as the red tail-lights bumped up and down along the narrow lane. Finally, they winked out of sight. Gwen said, "Good kids."

"Aye, good kids," Fenny agreed, sighing. Gwen kissed her husband, then turned and went back inside the house, taking her usual seat beside the fire.

Fenny's gaze lingered along the dark lane for a few more seconds. At last he closed the door on the winter and followed after Gwen, taking his favourite seat next to his wife.

"They're good souls, aren't they?" he asked.

Gwen smiled. "It's my belief that those four kids are as honest as you think they are, and yes, we can trust them. I'm certain of it."

Fenny nodded. "Me too," he said. Fenny took a sip of beer from his favourite tankard... the one with a goat head etched into a pentagram. "Merry Christmas, my love," he said.

"Merry Christmas, Fenny."

Later that evening, after Gwen had gone to bed,

Fenny made his customary late night visit to the barn. He unlocked the heavy doors and stepped inside, then locked the doors behind him. Without turning on any lights he walked over through the darkness to the fireplace altar. Reaching inside, he removed a brick, slid his hand into the recess, and pressed a button. A gentle hissing sound disturbed the otherwise silent space, and he stepped back. Reaching down, Fenny slid the ornamental rug away from the altar, revealing a wooden trap door. With the pneumatic locks released, he easily lifted the trap door and rested it gently against the brick work.

Then, and as he had done almost every evening since he'd lived at the old farm, he descended the stone steps into the secret chamber below. This subterranean space looked nothing like the area directly above. In fact, the barn above was a relatively new addition, built in the sixties by the Drayton family once they'd purchased the land from the farmer who owned it previously.

The walls here were not the rough stone walls of the barn above. These were smooth yellow sandstone, rendered to a fine finish and adorned with a series of painted motifs and intricate carvings. Around the walls stood tastefully-lit glass cabinets, and between those cabinets, ornate marble pilasters supported the roof, which of course was the floor of the barn above.

In the cabinets, which only a very select few

people had ever been allowed to see, was the greatest collection of Templar treasure anywhere on the planet. Magnificent Templar swords. Priceless multicultural artefacts from the Holy Land. Dazzling golden chalices. Parchments. Coins. Royal seals. Weapons from conquered enemies. Mamluk regalia. Hundreds and hundreds of artefacts that, if ever valued, would be worth a staggering amount of money, though they would forever remain priceless.

In pride of place, however, right in the centre of the high-tech, temperature-controlled room, was a shimmering suit of armour, complete with a shield bearing the iconic red cross of the Templars; la *croix pattée,* or the footed cross. It sat atop a stone block, taken from the original Temple of Solomon. It had been brought back to England after the second Crusade in 1148, as a sign that the city of Jerusalem was not infallible, and would indeed one day fall to the crusading armies of Europe, despite the failure of that Crusade. That it had ended up in this place in particular was not an accident. It exactly marked the geographical centre of England. Thus, it was emblematic of the Knights Templar of England's steadfast desire that the heart of their beloved nation, and the rule of their King, would never, ever be taken.

Beneath that suit of armour, a small golden plaque was set into the floor in front of the stone from the Temple of Solomon. The carved script read:

**The suit of armour of our fallen Brother,
James de Somervila
Lest we never forget.**

Fenny Drayton admired the armour for a few moments, lingering over the dents and scratches. As he always did, he let his imagination wonder about what it must have been like for his ancestors all those hundreds of years ago. He also thought of Steven Stalbridge, and felt only sadness. Of course, Steven could not be held responsible for the actions of his ancient ancestor, the traitor, Stephen de Stapelbrigg. He had simply believed the wrong story. Whether he was to learn the truth of it all now rested in another man's hands. And Fenny thought he knew what Hiram Kane would choose to do with that truth.

Fenny's order didn't keep the treasure there for selfish reasons, though Fenny couldn't deny it was a privilege to live in such close proximity to it, and an honour to be its keeper. It was here because their secret had to be kept at any and all cost. If they ever wanted to transport the treasure, or donate it to a museum, it risked exposing their secret headquarters. Questions would be asked, and they couldn't afford to let that happen. Under any circumstances, both the treasure, and their secret, must remain hidden from the world.

Taking his handkerchief from his pocket, Fenny wiped at a small smudge on the chest plate of the armour. Satisfied he'd removed it, he placed the cloth back in his pocket.

After one more glance around the room, Fenny ascended the stairs, closed the hatch and returned the rug to its original position. Then he engaged the powerful pneumatic locks once more.

He left the barn, locked the doors and returned to his house, safe in the knowledge that he had again done his duty, and that the secrets of The Silent Knights had been kept safe for at least one more revolution of the sun and the moon.

HOPES DASHED

Worn out from the last few days of travel and drama, Hiram, Alex, Evan and Luke piled out of the rental car and walked the last few hundred yards of their journey. They were all eager to get out of the cold and into the ancient cosy pub, equally eager to slug down a few Christmas Eve pints.

Throughout the hour of the drive back from Fenny Drayton, however, Hiram's mind had been swirling.

He'd learned so much in the last couple of days. Much of it was historical knowledge about the Templars, which was always fascinating. And yet, he'd also learned stuff he wasn't supposed to know, like the fact descendants of the Templars were alive and well and hiding secrets, potentially vital secrets, in preventing a major religious situation between Europe and the Islamic world.

Knowledge is power. It was a well-known phrase, and Hiram now had knowledge which in the wrong hands could be incredibly valuable.

He felt torn. He would never betray the promise he'd made to the Templar brothers from Silbury Hill, James and John. Not to mention their father, Fenny Drayton. And yet, didn't the world have a right to know that the Templars still existed? Didn't people deserve to know the truth about what had happened back in the early fourteenth century? And didn't he have a duty to share that knowledge with historians? His government?

Whenever Hiram ever had any doubts about what to do in certain situations, he always thought of his grandfather, Hiram Snr. *What would granddad do?* he asked himself. And that's what he did now. He asked himself what his granddad would do with this knowledge. The answer was simple. He would do nothing. He would honour his promise. He would never again mention what they had seen and heard and learned. He would keep his silence.

In the end, Hiram decided it was not his duty to share that knowledge, nor did he believe he had the right to. They were good men, James and John. As was the vicar, Ian, and Mary, from the church in Stow Longa. Fenny and Gwen Drayton were good people. All of them had dedicated their lives to keeping their secrets from the world. Hiram was not going to betray any of them. He had been asked if he would keep their secret, asked if he would remain silent about what he had learned.

He would. He was not a knight. But he would always remain silent about this.

"Ah, the wanderers have returned," yelled Steven Stalbridge from his familiar perch at the end of the bar. "Just in time for me to buy you all a Christmas ale."

Hiram and the others joined Steven at the bar, hoping he wouldn't ask them if they'd found anything interesting about his ancestor on their so-called grail quest, which, of course, was actually his grail quest. That's what they hoped. None of them were surprised when, even before their pints were poured, he asked his first questions.

"So how did it go? Did you... um, have fun?"

"Yes, we had a lot of fun, thank you," Alex answered. "It was a nice road trip to some interesting, er, places."

"Oh yes? Please, do tell me where you've been."

"Well," Hiram joined in. "After visiting Saint Giles church, we explored some interesting caves in Shropshire."

"Then we went south to have a look around the ancient monuments in Wiltshire," Evan added, "including the amazing stone circles at Avebury, and Silbury Hill."

"Yeah, then we headed north east and had a look

around the village of Stow Longa," Luke chimed in, "then ended up in a nice little place called... Fenny Drayton. We, um, saw some goats."

"Goats? Fenny Drayton? That's my ancestors name," Steven said.

"Yes, goats," said Evan. "But we think, um, Drayton... well, it's just a place name. A small village."

Steven didn't respond at first. He desperately wanted to learn more. Finally he spoke again. "Is that it?" Steven persisted. "Did you meet, um, any interesting people? Or find out about, you know, my famous heroic Templar ancestor?"

Hiram and the others sipped nervously at their pints. This was the moment they'd been dreading. The poor guy was desperate for some kind of clarification that his ancestor, who he believed to be named Drayton, was a heroic Templar Knight. The truth, unfortunately, was very different.

His ancestor, Stephen de Stapelbrigg, was a traitor of the highest order. He had betrayed his Templar brothers for nothing more than a bag of coins. Brave, loyal men that he had fought alongside in the Crusades, and whom he had shared his life with for so many years. He had betrayed them, knowing it would get them tortured and killed. And all because of his greed.

That greed had resulted in him having his head cut off and displayed in a tree. It was a shameful, pitiful and inglorious death, since which, the name

Stapelbrigg has forever been associated with betrayal and treachery.

It was the very opposite of what Steven believed. Hiram didn't have the heart to ruin that belief.

"Come on, kids, please tell me what you learned?" Steven was almost pleading.

"I'm really sorry," Hiram said, "but it was just a wild goose chase after all. We didn't learn anything."

"Nothing at all? Really?" Steven looked crestfallen.

"We're sorry. We really are."

Steven nodded, trying to put a brave face on his disappointment. "Well, I thank you for trying. I thank all of you. I guess I'll have to continue being plain old Steven Stalbridge for a little while longer, eh?"

"That's the spirit," Hiram said.

Steven nodded. "Merry Christmas, one and all, he bellowed, "Merry Christmas. Right, who wants another pint?"

And they all did.

EPILOGUE

ALL IS CLEAR, ALL IS BRIGHT

A month had passed and Hiram, Alex, Evan and Luke had resumed their studies back at the University of East Anglia in Norwich. True to their word, none of them had ever mentioned what had transpired just before Christmas again. They had more or less forgotten it, or had at least managed to put it out of their minds.

Hiram had brought a new car. Much to Evan's disgust it was another Mini Clubman estate, just as he'd promised. It was a newer model at least, and Evan had approved of the colour, a more subtle black instead of the ghastly beige of the previous iteration. It was still a mistake as far as Evan was concerned. Hiram had money... why the hell didn't he spend some of it on a decent car? None of them had discussed what had happened to Hiram's first car, and when asked why he'd changed vehicles, he'd just told them he was sick of the colour. Having seen it, none of them were surprised.

It was almost as if none of the dramatic events from before Christmas had ever happened. Almost.

But Hiram had changed. They had set out on what Evan had labelled a ridiculous 'grail quest', and although never speaking of it since, it was something none of them would ever forget. And yet for Hiram it had had a profound affect on his outlook for the future.

He absolutely loved his degree. He respected and admired all his professors, especially the inspirational Professor John O'nians. He had made a few lifelong friends over his years of study at the University of East Anglia's School of World Art Studies and Museology, and had developed as a person as well as gaining so much fascinating knowledge.

He was in his final year of a Masters course in anthropology, art history and archaeology, but had been focusing on the archaeology aspect for his final thesis. Hiram had always believed he wanted to be an archaeologist, and had enjoyed every minute of his time on various archaeological dig sites around the country. He'd even been on a couple of field trips abroad, in France and Turkey.

But their adventure in December, following the clues and relishing that sense of discovery, had made him reconsider everything. Yes, he loved archaeology. Yet now he firmly believed he preferred the idea of hunting things down than the act of digging them up. His great-grandfather had been a famous explorer. His grandfather too, though now he was in semi-retirement and working for the British Museum. His own father had never been interested in that kind of adventurous life. Those genetics had skipped him and landed squarely with Hiram.

Now it was clear. He was so close to finishing his Masters degree, just a few months before submitting his thesis to his professor, the legendary John Haines, a man he idolised. But his decision was made. He wasn't going to complete his masters degree.

He wouldn't need it anymore. Everything he'd already learned would stand him in good stead. He knew his decision would shock his family, though he believed his granddad would understand. It was going to disappoint his lecturers and especially Professor Haines. But again, Hiram thought, he would at least understand.

He knew his girlfriend Alex would be disappointed. Not disappointed in him for quitting his degree. Alex was as strong-willed as Hiram was, and if he'd made that decision it would have been for a good reason. They'd been getting closer and closer over the last few weeks and months, and had more or less moved in together, though it was still unofficial.

He was in love with Alex, no doubt about it. He wasn't sure if she felt the same, but that was okay with Hiram. They'd only known each other since last year, but he had never met anybody like her. He didn't like the idea of disappointing the woman he loved. But his decision was made.

Hiram had decided to leave. Not only would he leave university and his rented flat in Norwich, but he would be leaving the country completely. Hiram had decided to relocate to his favourite city, Cuzco, high in the Peruvian Andes. Once there he would set up an adventure company. He was going to lead expeditions into the Andes Mountains, an area of outstanding natural beauty and rich cultural history that he'd visited with his granddad when he was a teenager. He had loved that experience, and had always known he'd return. He didn't expect it to be so soon. He thought he might call the company *Hike of the Condor*.

It was all so clear now. His brief taste of the excitement of the quest back in December, that hint of danger, the thrill of the chase and that surge of adrenalin when successfully following those clues... it was all so clear.

He was going to be an adventurer. And one goal had made itself very clear already, so clear in fact it was almost an obsession.

He, Hiram Kane, was going to find the true lost city of the Incas, Vilcabamba.

THE END

(but please turn the page)

LIKE THAT? THEN YOU'LL LOVE THESE!

Book 0 — Silent Knight: Origin Story
Book 0.5 — The Golem of Prague
Book 1 — The Tiger Temple
Book 2 — The Samurai Code
Book 3 — The Condor Prophecy
Book 4 — The Shadow of Kailash
Book 5 — The Feathered Serpent
Book 6 — Of Curses and Kings
The Hiram Kane Box Set #I
The Hiram Kane Box Set #2

The Ryan Bodean Action Thrillers

Havana Fury
Atlantis Storm
Hemingway Found
Eldorado Gold
The Ryan Bodean Box Set 1-4

The Alexandria Ridley Vigilante Thrillers

Book 1 - I, Survivor

COLLABORATIONS

The Liberator Thrillers with Luke Richardson

Set Him Free

Set You Free

Set Them Free

Set Me Free

Apocalyptic Thrillers with Jay Tinsiano

ARK: Outbreak

Vigilante Media Thrillers with Edie Kaufman

Day of the Dead

Literary Fiction by me, Steven Moore

I Have Lived Today: A Boy's Coming of Age Story

YOUR REVIEW CAN MAKE A HUGE DIFFERENCE

Reviews are so helpful to an author, and they give us both the platform and the confidence to continue doing what we love. As an independently published author, I don't have the luxury of being backed by a big publishing house, so I have to rely on the quality of my writing, the ability of my stories to move people, and the generosity of my readers.

More importantly, however, reviews serve you, the reader, and readers like you. They help inform a potential reader if they're buying a book they will like, so they can spend their hard-earned money with confidence.

Thus, if you leave an honest review, everyone's a winner.

So if you enjoyed The Tiger Temple, I'd be very grateful if you could spend just a couple of minutes leaving an honest review on the book's Amazon page.

Please review **Silent Knight** now, by typing this link into your web browser:

https://geni.us/SilentKnight

Thank you very much,
Steven

PS...

Turn the page for a taster of the next bestselling Hiram Kane book in the series, ***The Tiger Temple.***

THE TIGER TEMPLE - A SAMPLE

It had been three long nights and three even longer days.

At night, at least they were kept focused by the surges of adrenalin brought on by fear of the unknown dangers lurking within the darkness, and the very real possibility of death; either their own, or of that they hunting.

They didn't want to kill it. The creature was worth a lot more to them alive. But if it came down to a choice between its life or theirs, then it was an easy choice to make.

The nights — and their minds — were filled with all the innate fears felt by most humans for tens of thousands of years; things out in the darkness they could hear but couldn't see, but whose silent bites could lead to excruciating pain, often paralysis... sometimes death.

There were those who believed the ancient rainforest was haunted by spirits, and the men were as fearful of those spirits as they were of the natural threats all around them. Perhaps, even, more fearful than they were of their boss.

The men were well and truly on edge, and every one of them wanted it to be over soon.

That is, except one man.

Not their boss. Their leader was different, cut from a very different cloth. Small yet fearless. Quiet, yet his silence could be deafening for those who worked for him. To some people, his nickname suggested arrogance. His manner suggested total control over all at mercy. They were only wrong about the arrogance, because a man who wielded as much psychological power over his people as he did simply didn't need arrogance. He only needed to be.

They called him Jago... The Rooster. And any man who'd ever dared cross The Rooster paid dearly... usually the ultimate price.

The Rooster was as clinical as he was cold. As callous as he was calm. You didn't get to become the most feared gang leader in all Java if you couldn't back it up with action, and The Rooster had backed his reputation up many times over.

Jakarta was a city of thieves and thugs, of conmen and killers... and The Rooster was the very best — and worst — of them all, rightfully rising to the pinnacle of Jakarta's notoriously dark underworld.

But Jago wasn't in the steaming God-forsaken jungles of northern Sumatra for the scenery. Nor was he there to visit his new hotel in Bukit Lawang, built after the devastating tragedy in 2003, when a flash flood roared through the sleepy riverside village killing hundreds and destroying everything in its path. That hotel, and others like it, were just businesses. Jago seized on the tragedy, and it had made him a fortune. But it gave him no pleasure. Men like The Rooster needed more than money to get a hard on for life.

The reason The Rooster was in the rainforest was not to make money, nor was it play with the fucking mosquitoes...

He was there to hunt.

And he would not leave empty handed.

Dusk had descended and gone with such speed that darkness it seemed was upon them almost instantly. And with that darkness came those same fears that stalked them every night.

It wasn't the only thing that stalked them.

Of course, they were there for the riches of the hunt. To the men a failed hunt would mean not only having to face the wrath of their master, The Rooster. It meant they might lose their job, or worse. They had to have success. To achieve that success they had to find and capture the king of this jungle. That was, if it didn't kill them first.

Though they hadn't seen it — they hadn't had a single sighting in three days and three nights — it had seen them.

The beast stood silently, its massive chest rising and falling with deep exhales and inhales. Its eyes were open wide, extracting as much help as it could from the residual light of the vanquished day. Its whiskers twitched, senses on full alert. Its paws were huge, their imprints in the soft ground of the jungle like craters. It stood upwind of the hunters' camp, thousands of years of survival instincts innately leading it to wait where it was safe. Yet it was never really safe when humans thought — foolishly — they owned the jungle.

But the magnificent creature's hunger dictated its actions. It always had, and it always would. That hunger dictated to him now.

Jago, The Rooster, was high on meth-amphetamines. He never drank alcohol, and in his day to day life in the shadows and lights of Jakarta, he never did drugs. But here in this vast, ancient rainforest of northern Sumatra he needed to be on high alert. Success on hunts like this were rare. Mistakes could be deadly. Sure, they almost always managed to kill some breed of animal. But that killing was just for sport. For fun. To quell the boredom.

But getting his hands on the real prize — preferably alive — well, that was so rare it made those unlikely successes unimaginably lucrative. The Rooster had only achieved that kind of success once before. It was a few years ago now, almost a decade, but it was the final push he'd needed to cement his position at the very pinnacle of the gangster food chain in all Java.

He'd succeeded on the hunt that season. They'd caught their quarry and a week later had sold it for huge profit. This time it was different. This time he didn't need the profit. He no longer needed the several hundred thousand dollars it would bring him. No, this time it was a status symbol he desired. This time they weren't going to sell the spoils of the hunt.

Jago was there to hunt the rare and endangered Sumatran tiger. But he was going to capture it, alive, and keep it for his pet.

The men sat still, staring out into the impossibly dark jungle. Nothing stirred. The breeze off the wide river nearby had dropped, and the trees no longer whistled. A stream softly gurgled twenty feet behind them. Birds roosted high above, and even the incessant drone of a billion insects had fallen silent.

Something was happening. While Jago's men held their breaths in fear, The Rooster himself felt alive. This was it. The moment he'd waited years for, anticipated, dreamed of.

The moment he'd always known was his.

The master of the jungle's heart began to race, pumping the blood faster through its powerful muscles, readying itself for the attack. Ready to kill.

Its nostrils flared, delicate bursts of moisture spraying invisibly into the humid air. The lowest of rumbles emanated from deep within its mighty chest, too quiet for the men to hear but loud enough to send a large toad bounding away to the safety of the stream. Eyes widened to their maximum. Breaths, deeper still.

The beast crouched. Poised. Huge hind legs coiled like lethal springs. And it sprang. It sprang with so much power it cleared the stream in one huge bound, bushes and small trees splintering before it as the beast crashed toward the humans.

It felt a moment's confusion, as they didn't move or cry out or run or turn and fire their weapons. The tiger had seen that before and expected it now. But it didn't come, and just as the massive jungle lord set to leap and slaughter the nearest intruder to its realm, the beast plummeted into an unseen pit, and hit the ground with a terrible, earth-shuddering thud and shattering a front leg. It lay there winded, wounded, confused. A moment later, before it could even stand and attempt to leap to safety, Jago shot him with enough tranquilliser to take down a beast three times its size.

The Rooster lowered the tranq gun and stared down into the dark pit. He'd had his men dig it months before, then cover it. No one ever came to this part of the jungle. He knew it would never be discovered. Equally, the tiger wouldn't know of it, wouldn't understand it if it did.

He stared down now, eyes wild with adrenalin and the delicious rush of power he felt at his dominion over everything in his world. First it was the classmates in school. Next, his older siblings. His father. His competitors. His city. And now, this jungle and its master were defeated, the beast lying at his feet, bested, subdued, and subservient to the new King of Sumatra.

The Rooster had achieved his desire. And Indonesia's underworld would soon know all about it.

Incense hung thick in the air, its bluish-grey haze adding to the somewhat mystical atmosphere. In the temple's inner sanctum, the organic frangipani scent synonymous with religious ceremonies in the village of Nyuh Kuning permeated every corner.

From somewhere out of sight, the haunting melodic chimes of the *rindik* musicians added a second layer of mystique. Coupled with the unique architecture, and shrine after shrine laden with flowers and offerings, Hiram Kane was again reminded that Bali truly was the 'Island of the Gods'.

Standing beside Hiram were Ketut and Putu, two brothers who had become his close friends since he'd arrived in their village almost three months previous. Ketut was lean, clean cut and good looking, and a popular resident of the community of eight-hundred that called Nyuh Kuning home. His shaggy hair gave him the appearance of a twenty-eight-year-old teenager, and Kane teased him for being the long-lost fifth member of The Beatles.

Putu was the older brother at thirty-seven. He was taller and broad shouldered, and handsome in a rugged way, but with watchful eyes and an air of menace about him he was acutely aware of and that had served him well in his younger years. The shaved head and huge tattooed biceps enhanced the look. And yet, despite his tough appearance Putu was lively, quick with a smile, and the type of man who would do anything for anyone. Sadly, that was often to his own detriment.

The physical difference between the siblings was stark, and Ketut's flip-flops were no match for Putu's heavy biker boots. But the love between the brothers was there for all to see. Their mutual respect was genuine and inspiring to Hiram, who, since he'd got to know them better over the last few months, had come to trust the brothers as if they were his own kin.

The colourful ceremony at the *pura puseh*, the 'Temple of Origin' located in the east of the village, thus nearer to the spiritually important Mount Agung volcano, was to honour the Balinese Hindu God *Betara Desa*. The annual event was a social highlight of the community, when the men got together to complain about taxes, the cost of scooter fuel and their aching joints, and the women got together to complain about the men. There was, of course, a lot of praying.

Hiram wasn't a religious man, but he'd always been fascinated by religion, a dissonance he was comfortable with. It gave him a chance to witness beautiful art and architecture, and visit peaceful, atmospheric ceremonies and temples such as this.

The three men stood to the rear of the temple. The brothers focused on the words of the priest, while Hiram watched with fascination as everyone present paid their respects to Betara Desa. Even the effervescent children were still and quiet, their attention where it was supposed to be. Hiram felt a deep respect for the serene and innate discipline so evident in Balinese people.

Gazing through the swirling incense clouds and the throng of bodies, he caught a glimpse of a young girl, who happened to turn and catch his eye. Her mischievous smile would have melted any heart, and Hiram had a momentary pang of regret he'd decided not to have kids of his own. But as always, it was gone in a flash. Hiram knew that the adventurous, spontaneous lifestyle he enjoyed and the scrapes he all too often found himself in, plus the dangerous overpopulating of the planet, meant not having kids was one of the few sensible decisions he'd ever made. Besides, he'd yet to convince the long-term yet unrequited love of his life, the beautiful art historian Alexandria Ridley, to even commit to a relationship. So no, Hiram loved kids, but he would leave producing them to other people.

He recognised the pretty little girl in the jade green dress... Ayu? She turned away, but before she did she poked her tongue out at him. He promptly returned the compliment. Before she disappeared back into the crowd the last thing Hiram saw was the stuffed toy tiger that had seemed permanently attached to her hand since he'd first seen her around the village.

Crack. Crack. Crack.

The unmistakable retort of gunshots echoed

around the temple, but an instant later the place had fallen silent as the worshippers processed the shocking sounds.

A moment later the place erupted in a chaotic chorus of screams and shouts and a crush of bodies as the terrified villagers scrambled towards the exit. Before he could react Hiram felt himself forced back against the inner wall, unable to resist the manic surge of bodies and the flailing arms of the fear-stricken worshippers. Forced back into the same corner, Ketut locked eyes with his friend. Shock and fear were written on his face, his wild eyes telling their own story.

The screaming and surging continued as close to three-hundred people hustled to safety, the unknown gunman still elusive.

"What the hell's going on?" Hiram shouted to Ketut, who remained speechless. "Are you hurt?"

Ketut shook his head, his mouth agape.

"Ketut? Are you injured?" he pressed.

"No... no. I am okay. Where... Where is Putu?"

Hiram glanced among the hordes, finally thinning as the majority of temple goers had at last made it outside.

"I can't see him," Hiram yelled above the still rowdy bedlam. "Let's get out of here."

They joined the last stream of villagers, acutely aware there may still be a gunman in the temple, when Hiram's ears pricked up at the most pitiful wailing he'd ever heard. It was a woman, crying out for... for Ayu?

"Where is my daughter? Where is Ayu?" she howled in her native Balinese. Recognising that final word, Hiram was instantly on high alert. He glanced at Ketut, who had also heard those dreadful cries. With horror Hiram remembered Ayu was Ketut's niece.

With single-minded determination Ketut forced his way through the crowds and burst outside, the sudden bright sunlight momentarily blinding him.

Hiram joined him seconds later, and a moment after that Putu arrived. The man was panic-stricken.

"Where is Ayu?" he bellowed. "Where is my niece?"

Just then the ascending growl of powerful motorbike engines thundered above the hum of the crowd. Hiram swivelled upon hearing that roaring chaos, turning in time to witness a scene he would never forget; little Ayu being shoved roughly onto a motorbike seat and clamped between the legs of a man. After catching Hiram's eye and holding that glare for a few seconds, the big man pulled down his blacked-out visor and accelerated away from the temple, two other huge bikes right on his tail and scattering bewildered worshippers in all directions.

Without a second's hesitation Hiram grabbed the brothers. "With me. Now!"

Neither Ketut nor Putu had seen what their

friend had witnessed, but they knew him well enough by now not to doubt him. As he sprinted off to the rear of the temple towards their own motorbikes, they followed. Less than fifteen seconds later the trio were tearing up the main road through Nyuh Kuning towards the sacred Monkey Forest, on what had suddenly turned into a rescue mission.

Enjoy this excerpt of the next Hiram Kane novel?

Buy **The Tiger Temple** NOW, by typing this link into your browser:

https://geni.us/TigerTempleAMS

Turn the page for a taster of the next bestselling Hiram Kane book in the series, ***The Samurai Code.***

THE SAMURAI CODE - A SAMPLE

Prologue

A battlefield near Kyoto, Honshu Island, Japan

April 25th 1185

A pair of ravens cawed and stabbed at each other with powerful beaks, their inky feathers glinting beneath a full moon as they scrapped over a torn hunk of flesh. Human flesh. So much human flesh.

Ghostly wraiths of mist sped across the near darkness as if blown by *Futen*, the Japanese god of the wind, and carried with them the pungent smell of rotting corpses. An icy chill did nothing to quell the sickening stench. Bodies lay strewn everywhere on the soggy, blood-stained earth, spilled guts and crushed bones bearing grim testimony to the recent battle.

For days, the main conflict of *Dan-no-ura* had raged in the inland sea not far from Kyoto, but the ground skirmishes were just as terrible, and thousands had died. And yet, although the fighting was over, the killing and dying was not.

An exhausted *Katsu Hanzō* stumbled, the physical and mental exertions of the battle edging him to the brink of collapse. Through bloodshot eyes, he scanned the battlefield, and saw acres of churned up ground laced with fallen samurai, both dead and dying. He was among the few survivors, though he didn't feel lucky. To die in battle was a great honour, as long as you died with dignity and courage. His own body had been sliced often, arms, back, and chest crisscrossed with near fatal wounds. Yet destiny had spared him, and he knew why; he had one last duty to fulfil.

He was hurting, though he would not show it — not in front of his enemy; the same enemy that had slaughtered his father and brother, their bodies somewhere to the south where the tide of the battle had finally turned in favour of the Minamoto, the hated samurai clan from the north who now encircled his master.

Twenty yards away Takamochi Taira stood defeated, the enemy closing in around him like a human noose. But it was okay. Takamochi knew what must be done. As his second in command, so did Katsu Hanzō.

The leader of the Taira clan took one last look around, his gaze resting on the young warrior. He bowed, long and slow, and Katsu returned the respect. Then Takamochi slowly dropped to his knees.

The ravens squabbled, their raucous calls piercing a suddenly silent world as he whispered poetic words heard by no one but himself.

I'm glad to die
in spring, beneath
Blossoms of cherry,
while a springtime moon
is full.

Takamochi carefully positioned his white kimono on the filthy ground before him, and readied himself, closing his eyes and slowing his breaths. He sensed his trusted kai-sha-ku-nin — his assistant — Katsu position himself alongside, and heard the metallic sound of his samurai sword being withdrawn from its sheath.

He opened his eyes for the final time, and pulled out his own short, ceremonial O'tanto dagger, its handle bound in leather. He admired the weapon, narrowing his eyes as his heart rate slowed. Calmly, Takamochi turned the blade towards his own stomach, and gripped hard.

It was time.

侍

CHAPTER 1

THE MUDDY WATER raged past him with such power the very ground shook, and it was all he could do to stop himself falling in and being swept to a violent death. And it wasn't just the filthy, swollen river that threatened. The rain hammered him like penny-sized bullets, the wind gusting like the breath of vexed, forgotten gods.

Had he been in the sanctuary of a stone building looking out, or even watching nature's barbaric display on a TV or movie screen, it would have been an amazing show. Horrific, yet amazing.

But Hiram Kane wasn't. Instead, he was braced on the busted banks of a rampaging river that carried along within its churning, broiling wake an eclectic collection of crumpled cars, twisted, fallen trees, wrecked wooden houses, and —

And bodies.

Scores of bodies.

But not all of them were dead. The gurgled half-screams reached him from all directions, and reverberated off the steep cliffs, some with frightening clarity, others a pitiful wail. The pleading voices sounded so close — and so many — like a tortured choir, but he just couldn't make out from which bobbing, floating bodies the sounds came, such was the ferocious intensity of the river.

He knew he had to act. And fast. There were others around him, more volunteers to aid the rescuers, but panic was the dominating emotion, and not enough was being done, people too afraid or shocked to help. Kane beckoned to a man clutching a rope who seemed frozen to the spot, anxiety crinkling his face. Kane didn't speak much Japanese, aside from basic greetings and asking directions. He could, of course, order a beer. But with a series of frantic hand gestures and an encouraging look, the man understood. Kane grabbed the rope and tied it, first around himself, then the other end to a fallen tree, whose exposed, gnarly roots gave evidence to the storm's mighty strength. Kane believed they would hold, and called on the other man to help reel him back in, like some kind of macabre human fishing trip.

"Tasukete! Tasukete!" came a cry from the river. Help! Help!

Kane's eyes darted upstream, and scanning the torrents, he caught a flash of red coming towards him amid the churning brown. An instant later, what looked like a red jacket suddenly disappeared. Kane cursed, but kept searching, and after several anxious seconds, it reappeared a dozen yards closer and nearer the bank. This was it.

He took a few steps back, and with an uncompromising look at his assistant, both to encourage himself and to make the man accountable, Kane took a running jump as far as he could into the deadly river.

The world turned black as he went under, the power and force of the flow greater than he could have imagined. He reached out a long leg, desperate to brace against something solid below, but the river was at its highest level for half a century, its surface a maelstrom twenty feet above normal. A strong swimmer and experienced scuba diver, Kane didn't panic, and with a flurry of powerful strokes he surfaced several yards upstream, right into the path of the onrushing little girl in red. Snagging her into his arms, her flailing limbs dragged them both under the surface. He choked on mouthfuls of the filthy river as he resisted the immense flow, the air and water expelled in dreadful, gagging spurts, but once again he broke the surface, just as the girl slipped into unconsciousness. Their bodies bumped and shuddered against the rapids, and swayed this way and that, first away from the bank then back again, and just as it looked as if they might finally reach the shore a fierce undercurrent sucked them away.

The man on the bank had planted his feet and was gamely hauling Kane in with all his strength. Soon joined by another man and woman who had seen what was happening, they pulled, the thirty yards of played-out rope now twenty. Fifteen. Now just five yards of rope were left, and the man looked into Kane's eyes, wide and hopeful over the frothing water. But then some invisible violence yanked Kane and the girl away yet again, the force of the shift almost wrenching the three helpers into the torrents themselves. In desperation, they managed to wedge themselves amongst the tangled roots of the ancient tree, and now secure, pulled on the rope as if it were their own child on the end. It was someone's child.

Yard by yard, inch by inch, Kane and the girl were hauled to the edge, and after what felt like ten minutes, but was less than three, the river finally relinquished its death grip and they were dragged onto the bank, the girl comatose and Kane gasping for air.

The woman who had helped with the rope took over with impressive authority. In what was the first luck of the day, she happened to be an off-duty paramedic who'd gone to the river to assist survivors. She knelt next to the girl, who looked no more than ten years old, and got right to work giving her the kiss of life.

Within seconds, the girl's lungs vomited the water out in a sludgy, brown spray, and another minute later, the woman's husband carried her to the nearby road where a series of ambulances waited to transport the storm's victims to hospital.

The man with the rope looked at the now recovered Kane and smiled. They shared a moment of gratitude and admiration, but it didn't last. They hadn't yet spoken a word to each other, but Kane was not surprised when the man looked into his eyes and said, in English, "Again?"

With a slow nod and the barest hint of a grin, Kane stood, and after scanning the troughs and swells of the roaring flash flood for human life, once more launched himself into its violence.

Over the course of the next three hours, Kane and Naki took turns risking nature's wrath in order to save the lives of eighteen men, women, and children. It was only after the surging flood waters had abated and the river had calmed to something like its usual, placid state that Kane and his new friend, their minds and bodies exhausted and battered from such a harrowing few hours, slumped down on their backs to rest.

Rescue support workers brought them blankets and steaming bowls of miso soup, which they ate in silence, neither with the energy nor desire to talk. But what was there to say? Both men had done what they had to do. Kane had not thought twice about putting his own life on the line to help others, and neither had Naki. It was just what good people did.

With nothing further they could do to help, Kane and Naki scrambled up the now destroyed banks of the Saba River, aware the worst of the flooding had passed, but also with the knowledge that landslides within the surrounding hills were a real and likely threat. Naki led Kane swiftly to his car, parked half a mile walk from the destruction zone, and convinced him to go with him to his home. As Kane's hotel was in the area now off-limits due to damage and the possible threat of further floods, he accepted the offer. Fifteen minutes later, Kane found himself in a hot shower, revitalised, safe from nature's fury, and grateful to be alive.

But Kane was devastated. They had helped save many people, but many more had perished, and tears of sadness and frustration fell as he took every loss personally.

Hiram Kane would have gladly traded his own life to save a few more from the river.

侍

Enjoy this excerpt of the next Hiram Kane novel?

Buy **The Samurai Code** NOW by typing this link into your browser:

https://geni.us/TheSamuraiCodeAMS

Turn the page for a taster of the next bestselling Hiram Kane book in the series, ***The Condor Prophecy*.**

THE CONDOR PROPHECY - A SAMPLE

Lima, Peru.

Summer, 2011

Light wind lifted dust from the dry grounds of the park, swirling it through the cool air, like memories drifting through time. Centuries of painful memories.

Parque de la Muralla was almost silent in the hours before dawn, the only sound the nattering of stray dogs aroused by the intruders. It was still night, but it wasn't very dark, Lima's garish street lights casting crazed shadows everywhere, one in particular, prominent across the ground; a Spanish conquistador astride his horse.

They didn't have long. Soon the park would bustle with early morning joggers, eager to exercise before the sun rose too high. Four men stood silently beneath a street lamp. They were young men, most in their early twenties, but were tough and wiry, their dark, chestnut skin and narrow eyes indicative of Quechuan mestizo men in Peru.

The gathered men were proud of what they had done and what they were going to do. Nevertheless, they didn't want to be caught, and had a lot more to achieve. They ran to that vast shadow and stopped, taking a moment to gaze up at the massive statue before them. It was tall, some twenty feet, its bronze glimmering in the darkness. The rider sat mounted on a powerful horse, he and it both heavily armoured. He had his sword raised, and the stern glare in his eyes would intimidate any enemy.

The statue's striking profile was a dark and dominant silhouette against the faint hint of dawn. Impressive. But not for long.

The first of the four men — their single-minded leader — clambered up the pedestal with a length of thick rope. He edged high onto the mighty horse's back, where the cast bronze shone under the lamp's orange glow. Two other men laced their own ropes around the front legs of the horse, pulling hard to tighten the knots. In less than two minutes, the statue of horse and rider had three lengths of heavy-duty rope dangling from it.

The fourth man edged their powerful flatbed truck into position, twenty yards in front of the statue. With all the ropes now linked as one, the driver fastened it to the truck's winch. It was time.

The leader, his authority unquestioned, motioned to the others to join him. They stood in line, and with the horse and rider statue before them, the big man said a few words in his native Quechuan:

ACROSS THE ANDES MOUNTAINS,
the mighty condor once soared,
Where spirits of the Incas
will look down forever more,
And when the name Pizarro,
from the history books has gone,
The legend of the Incas,
forever and always, will live on.

The youngest of the group at just twenty, the driver ran to the truck and restarted the engine, revving it to life. He stepped hard on the pedal, the screech of the wheels harsh on their ears. But they didn't care. The driver focused his eyes on the leader's raised arm and waited for the signal. Their hearts raced. The moment was near.

Destiny.

And then the arm fell.

He lifted his foot from the brake, and pressing the accelerator down with all his strength the powerful truck lurched backwards. The ropes resisted, the truck wheels skidding and swerving on the concrete, but it didn't retreat. The thick bronze of the statue groaned under the pressure as the eerie sound resonated across the empty park.

Then the rider's head shifted just a few inches

forwards as the statue began to yield. The driver gunned the pedal, straining the engine to its limit. And as if in slow motion, one of the horse's knees buckled, the entire statue tilting to the left. The screaming of tyres and twisting metal sounded deafening to the men standing close. Yet still the horse and rider didn't fall, but clung on as if their immortality depended on it. After long, nervous seconds, the men shared doubtful looks. But finally the second leg buckled, and the colossal sculpture fell to its knees. It left the rider leaning precariously forwards and the tip of his lance mere inches from the ground.

The leader looked at his driver, an instinctive message passing between them. His build was solid, and tall for an Andean native at six foot. The man commanded obedience. He was the eldest at thirty-two, but despite his relatively young age his weathered face was scarred and his eyes had already seen a lifetime of pain and disappointment.

The driver slipped the gears from reverse to first and as the truck edged forward a few yards the ropes fell slack. A heavy silence now haunted the empty park, the street dogs long since retreated in fear. After all the noise they'd made, the park wouldn't be empty for long.

This was it. The final effort. Their leader nodded, his wild eyes alive with anticipation. The driver took a deep breath, slammed the truck in reverse, and accelerating backwards the ropes pulled taut and the huge statue was unceremoniously hauled to the ground. As bronze slammed against concrete and sparks flew like an exploding firework, the horrific sound of warped and scraping metal was a fitting welcome to the dawning of a new era.

The driver left the truck and joined the others as they walked to the head of the fallen rider. They didn't speak, but they didn't need to. Their duty was done. The prophecy was being fulfilled.

The men turned toward the truck, but the leader paused. After a moment's thought, he walked back to the rider's caved in head. Unzipping the fly of his jeans, and with utter calm, the big man urinated on the upturned face. Satisfied, he rejoined the others.

Without a word they drove away into the night, just as the day's first locals began entering the park. And the men left safe in the knowledge that the despised Spanish conquistador Francisco Pizarro would never cast his dark shadow over Inca lands again.

MAY 7TH, 2012

THE ANDES MOUNTAINS

Hiram Kane swatted half-heartedly at a mosquito. It's not that they didn't drive him insane. They did, the very bane of his life. But something else occupied his thoughts in that moment, and not even the buzzing of a million mosquitoes would distract him.

He sat on a flat rock, the ancient stone warmed from a high, midday sun. A nearby waterfall churned white, gravity sending it cascading into the valley below, its constant white-noise roar transcending all other sound. But Hiram heard nothing. He sat still and focused, his mind tuned into something the few people sitting nearby couldn't have known. Squinting against the harsh light, he stared into the jungle before him, narrowed eyes penetrating the impenetrable.

He was close. He knew it, could feel it in his bones.

The quest of a lifetime — the quest of several lifetimes — would at last be over. Kane had found what he and so many others before him had sought. It was within his grasp, and as electricity tingled his fingertips Hiram knew he'd found the real lost city of the Incas.

Vilcabamba.

Kane and his team members were deep in Peru's iconic Sacred Valley, far from the overused hiking trails between Machu Picchu and the city of Cuzco. Few foreigners in the modern era ever laid eyes on the wild terrain in that unexplored area of the valley, which meant the scenery was untainted by humans, thus remained magnificent. Mountains towered off at impossible angles in every direction. Some peaks were covered in snow, despite the warmer season, while others lay shrouded beneath an almost perpetual mist. It lent them a mystical quality always so alluring to Hiram. The steep, jungled slopes fell away to the mighty Urubamba River, where its dark and dangerous waters raged in violent brown rapids.

Kane had been close to the area before. The last time was twelve months previous, when he'd led another expedition of archaeologists and wide-eyed treasure hunters far into the depths of the valley. Most people didn't really believe they would find the genuine lost city of Vilcabamba, but it didn't stop them dreaming of success, and groups dedicated vast amounts of time and money every year to try. It was Hiram Kane's job, and pleasure, to lead them.

But Kane differed from the others, and always had. Hiram truly believed the legend of Vilcabamba was real, and not only that, but he would be the man to find it. And he had an advantage over all those others.

Hiram Kane had a map.

A contemplative frown pinched Kane's face as he pondered his decision, his eyes darkened by deep thought and his mouth set in what looked like a scowl but was more a study in concentration. He had a big choice to make, and he would not take it lightly.

Considered average looking by most, and not least himself, Kane possessed a rugged, outdoorsy quality admired by many. At a modest five feet eleven but with a physique that hinted at his years of competitive sport and outdoor living, Kane cut a commanding presence. Kane was reserved by nature, yet his cropped and slightly greying brown hair and perma-stubble added a tough edge. But his rich hazel eyes–eyes that faded to jade green under a bright sun–were sharp and wise and painfully honest. With a few hidden tattoos and a collection of well-earned scars, Kane's was a body that had seen and felt a fully lived life. He'd even lost half a finger, destroyed by a bullet when he found himself confronted by ruthless Yakuza men in Japan last year. It still hurt sometimes, a painful reminder of that horrific episode on Miyajima Island.

Yet, Kane would be the first to tell you he was only now getting started. Life's short, he said often, seize it by the horns. On his expeditions, he led by example.

But Kane felt torn. The group of six people with him, resting in the shade of a native polylepis tree after a long and arduous hike up the valley, had all invested a lot to join this expedition, and every one of them had the same ambitions as Hiram; locate the lost city of the Incas. They all wanted to be there when history got rewritten, wanted to be there when the true Vilcabamba was discovered.

They deserved to know the truth, of course. All six were successful in their respective fields, and among them were two archaeologists, two art historians, an eminent professor of antiquities, and a photographer. Completing the team were three porters, four mules, and a cook. Despite the heat and the harsh conditions, the native Quechuan fellows had barely raised a sweat. They sat away from the group, quietly savouring their rolled cigarettes while chewing wads of bitter coca leaves. In contrast, the foreigner's clothes were soiled, their bodies drenched in sweat, and their overworked lungs gasped for rarified breath in the high altitude air, the very epitome of exhaustion. Yet, no matter their physical state, all eyes were wide with wonder at the imposing panoramas that very same altitude granted them.

He should share his thoughts with them. They had that right. Kane though had always worried that if the wrong people found out about Vilcabamba, then the world's press would descend upon the site too soon and before the proper provisions and precautions were in place. Yes, these guys were all professionals. But that didn't guarantee they would act in a professional manner. In fact, Kane believed in many cases it almost guaranteed they wouldn't.

Kane was just being cautious, and he understood he had to tell them what he was thinking. After all, they had each paid him a small fortune based on the reputation of his integrity.

Now rested, a lean, middle-aged archaeologist from Cornell called out to Kane. "What do you see in there, Hiram? Not a mountain lion, is it?" He chuckled at his own joke. No one else did.

Kane swivelled to face them. It was time to tell them what he believed was true; that beyond the near jungle, just a few hours hike from where they were sitting, lie the place that had ruined so many fortunes, shattered so many dreams, and over the last century, had cost many, many lives. Yes, they were just a couple of miles from the fabled lost Incan city. Vilcabamba.

"No, it's not a puma," Kane said with a smile in

his deep, confident tone. "That would be exciting though, wouldn't it?"

"Well, what is it, man?" the archaeologist asked, impatience lacing his voice. "What's kept you so rapt for the last fifteen minutes?"

"When we set off on this mission," said Kane, "we each dreamt of what we'd find. Well, it's my honest opinion that a few —"

Suddenly, the docile mules began braying while straining hard at their tethers, causing a commotion among the Quechuans. Something was wrong. The mules knew it, and hearing their ominous cries, so did the porters. In thick, accented Spanish, their leader, a short but commanding figure, shouted, "Carrera! Carrera!" Run! Run!

A low roar emanated from deep within the very ground they sat on, a grinding rumble, like far-away thunder. The hairs on the back of the archaeologist's neck stood up, his intuitive fear instant. The tree above him swayed, its papery red bark trembling. And then the ground shook.

Earthquake.

The ground shook with violence — left to right, up and down — and those who'd jumped to their feet were thrown to the hard earth like scarecrows in tornado alley. Boulders of all sizes came tumbling toward them from high up the slopes, a loaf sized rock striking an unfortunate mule on the head and killing it on the spot. The polylepis creaked, the thick trunk splintering, and it fell, the Cornell archaeologist diving clear with inches to spare.

Without a moment's hesitation, Kane and his Quechuan leader sprang into action. They darted across the rocks and grabbed the two nearest members of the group, shoving the stunned senior art historian and the young photographer to the safety of a ledge. But with a deafening roar the ledge shifted, and like a slow-moving tsunami, it crumbled down the slope. "Landslide!" Kane shouted, "Move. Now!"

Two of them leapt clear, the professor of antiquities and the younger archaeologist. The French art historian immediately followed. However, her young PhD student companion Claude froze in fear, rooted where he stood. She shouted, "Allez, Claude, se dépêche!" Come on! Hurry!

But Claude didn't move.

In the dozens of expeditions he'd led before, Kane had never lost anyone. There'd been many earthquakes, a common event in the Andes, and plenty of landslides, and Kane had witnessed stronger ones than this. But he knew things could worsen, and probably would. Using all his athleticism he scrambled down a few yards, almost riding the loose debris, until he straddled the fallen tree, and leapt across the crevice that opened between Claude and the group.

"Claude," he yelled. "You need to move."

"Ce n'est pas possible! I... I can not!" Terror shook his voice and tears streaked his dusty cheeks. But at that moment the sliding ledge came to a shuddering halt, the horrifying rumble fading to a direful growl. Kane took his chance.

"It's okay, my friend. You can do it. You have to move. Take my hand."

Claude shook his head, still unable to move. Then, just twenty yards away, a boulder the size of a small Citroen crashed past them, slamming trees aside like dominoes until it disappeared into the misty valley below. Claude was a sitting duck, and it was all the inspiration Kane needed.

Without pause he launched himself out onto the precarious ledge, only just finding his balance in time to prevent plummeting to a certain death. Then, and with some not-so-gentle physical persuasion and a few choice expletives, he hauled the young Frenchman over the crevice, almost certainly saving his life. The others, huddling under a tree and thanking their God or the universe that the earthquake had somehow stopped, stared at Hiram Kane in speechless awe.

Kane and his head guide, Sonco, hustled around the group checking for injuries, relieved to see they'd all escaped with little more than a few scratches and scrapes. They'd been lucky, Kane knew. He also knew they weren't out of trouble. After a quick deliberation with Sonco, who understood the terrain better than any man alive, they agreed another landslide might happen at any moment, and in fact they expected it. Kane addressed the group.

"We've had a narrow escape, but the danger hasn't passed. Earthquakes often have after-shocks, and it wouldn't take a lot for the whole side of this mountain to collapse. We have to go. Now! We'll backtrack as fast as we can in the direction we came for an hour, and there we'll make camp. If nothing drastic happens during the night, we can return tomorrow, and depending on the trails, try to continue on."

Every member of the group agreed without hesitation, especially Claude, whose tear-stained face nodded rapid approval. Even Mr Cornell didn't complain.

As they retreated to a safer distance along the trail, and both the real and proverbial dust had settled, Kane recalled he'd been on the verge of telling the others they were close to Vilcabamba.

He was not a religious man, far from it, but the rituals and traditions of the world's diverse civilisations fascinated Kane. He was also a touch superstitious, though he wouldn't admit it, and Hiram couldn't help but wonder if the landslide was a sign from the Incan Earth Goddess, Pachamama. The ancient Incas believed if they upset Pachamama, she had the ability to destroy the land with violent earthquakes–like the one they'd just witnessed. Hiram gave little credence to such archaic superstitions himself, but there it was. On the hike to camp the thought lingered with him.

Kane settled into a restless silence as he walked. After another consultation with Sonco, they believed they were now beyond any immediate danger, which meant tomorrow they could continue with the expedition. But it somehow didn't feel right. Kane was an instinctive man and had learned the hard way to trust those instincts. The one occasion he hadn't trusted them had haunted him for almost three decades. Shaking his head, he dismissed those dark thoughts and pushed on.

After arriving at their new campsite, Kane spent a couple of hours deliberating his options whilst the porters set up camp and the team members tried to relax after their harrowing near miss. It was a tough decision, but after once more conversing with his most trusted friend, Sonco, he made it. Kane was terminating the expedition.

It was a big call, but now he'd made it there was no backing down. Whatever had caused the earthquake and the subsequent landslide — whether an act of nature, or the supernatural whim of Pachamama, as Sonco suggested — Kane took it as a sign that one way or another he should keep the surety he felt about their proximity to Vilcabamba to himself. If confronted — if some of the party insisted they push on — he would inform them the terrain was too unstable, that it was too dangerous to proceed, and that he as expedition leader had a responsibility for their safety. If necessary, he'd remind them it was also in the contracts they'd all signed.

Kane was sorry it was over for them — he was sorry for himself, too — but there was no other choice. He would also tell them about Pachamama, about Incan superstitions, and hope they were superstitious enough to read into it the same inauspicious warning as him; that the Earth Goddess had chosen to keep the Inca secrets a mystery.

And though he himself didn't buy into it, Kane knew exactly how Sonco felt.

Anyone would be foolish to challenge Pachamama's will.

Enjoy this sample of the latest Hiram Kane book?

Buy The Condor Prophecy NOW by typing this link into your browser:

https://geni.us/TheCondorProphecyAMS

Turn the page for a taster of the next bestselling Hiram Kane book in the series, ***The Shadow of Kailash.***

THE SHADOW OF KAILASH - A SAMPLE

PROLOGUE

To Market

Mumbai, India

6:19 a.m.

"Move!" barked the massive overseer, his dark eyes devoid of all compassion. "Move. Now!"

Azim raised his hand as if to strike the young woman, who stood at the end of a line of fourteen others just like her. She flinched. It wouldn't be the first time he'd struck her; she wore the welts and bruises to prove it. But not on her face. The men never struck the girls' faces. It was bad form to damage the goods before potential buyers got to see them.

They filed out, a procession of withered, frightened and abused young women who not long ago were enjoying drinks with friends in one bar or another, only to have disappeared without warning. Not one of them were seen nor heard from since.

Of course, the girls weren't all acquired together. None of them knew each other, except the two French sisters, and each had gone missing at various stages over the course of the last few weeks. And they shared several characteristics in common. They were all young, between eighteen and twenty-five, and pretty. Very, very pretty. The last place each of them had been seen by friends or travel companions was a bar, though not the same one. And one more common trait they shared: they were all white. After all, 'The Vulture' had to meet his buyers' specific tastes, and only pretty young white-skinned girls fit the profile.

The Vulture looked on, impassive, as Azim shoved them forward, assisted by several of his men. The girls were silent, their distress muted both by fear and the powerful sedatives they'd unknowingly taken with their water. Herding them like cattle up the dank and dingy staircase, Azim threw open the door and led them out, the girls blinded by the sudden burst of dazzling dawn sunlight, the first they had seen or felt in many days, in some cases several weeks.

In the loading bay a shabby truck reversed, its warning siren piercing the heavy silence. It mattered little. The Vulture owned the dilapidated warehouse, and no one else would be around at five on a Sunday morning in that rundown, forgotten corner of old Mumbai.

One by one they shuffled on bound feet into the rear of the truck, too weak and too afraid to resist, resigned almost to whatever horrific fate awaited them. Except one woman. She was tall, and her piercing green eyes never left Azim's. He already knew this one was trouble.

Azim followed them in, shoving them forward, himself followed by two leering thugs, their filthy imaginations running wild. But they wouldn't touch the girls. Interfering with The Vulture's inventory would surely cost them their lives, theirs forfeit, worthless to him compared to these girls, who were priceless to the right client.

Azim glanced now at The Vulture, whose narrowed eyes stared unblinking at his cargo from the shadows. After a moment, and satisfied with his stock, he offered Azim the barest hint of a nod, which the big overseer returned before sliding down the back door of the truck and bolting it shut with a metallic clunk, locking the terrified girls inside with the lecherous henchmen. Azim jumped down from the loading dock, dusted off his suit, and climbed into the driver's seat of a classic Bentley Arnage 4.4, its bronze paintwork glimmering beneath an already hot sun.

Straightening his tie and smoothing down his bespoke Armani jacket, The Vulture slid down his

Gucci shades and descended the steps onto the loading bay and to his waiting car.

One of his men stepped forward and swung open the back door, and The Vulture climbed in and relaxed into the plush leather interior. He checked his Rolex.

"Ready, sir?" asked Azim without looking back.

The Vulture caught Azim's eyes in the rearview mirror, then glanced once more at his £15,000, 18-carat Everose gold Pearlmaster 39. The pure gold hands confirmed it was 6:30 am.

He smiled inwardly. "Yes, Azim. I am ready." He closed his eyes and took a deep breath. "It is time to take this meat to market."

THE CALM BEFORE

AGRA, INDIA

There were few moments in the history of Alexandria Ridley when she found herself genuinely lost for words. Quick-witted and incredibly sharp, Ridley could hold her own in any conversation and in any company and was always able to crack a joke in an instant, regardless of the situation. Nothing held Alex Ridley's tongue for long.

But after waiting in the pre-dawn cool of an Indian morning for what seemed an eternity, where she'd enjoyed jovial chatter over hot chai with dozens of tourists, both foreign and Indian alike, when she finally stepped through the impressive red-brick archway and gazed upon the incredible vista spreading out before her eyes, her breath caught in her throat. Few things silenced Alex Ridley. This did.

Never before in all her extensive world travels

had she lain eyes upon anything quite so magnificent. The graceful beauty of the scene, not to mention the unexpected size of the strangely delicate structure before her, mesmerised her and hastened her heartbeat. She was admiring perhaps the world's greatest ever monument built for love, and in that moment, while surrounded by equally mesmerised people from all across the world and from all walks of life, love is exactly what Ridley felt.

And with all her heart, Ridley was ready to love.

Standing beside her, Hiram Kane snuck a sideways glance at Ridley and smiled. She looked radiant in that faint morning glow, her almost-raven hair shimmering in the pale light and her blue eyes seemingly iridescent. Kane was in awe, not only of Ridley's beauty, but by the stunning vista. It was the same emotion he experienced on his first visit to Agra some twenty years before. On that occasion he'd stood spellbound, just as he remained spellbound now. Yet nothing made Kane happier than seeing Ridley enamoured this way, and he'd never seen her looking as at peace and happy as she seemed in that moment. His heart swelled too, and with his two loves nearby — Ridley, of course, and his most beloved example of architecture that remained the very definition of love just a couple of hundred yards away — Kane too had never been happier.

The sun had not yet risen fully, but enough light penetrated the complex to cause a wonderfully mystical, almost ethereal ambiance about the place. Ridley looked up at Kane, his tall athletic figure in silhouette but his eyes ablaze with the light of a million dreams, and a single, silvery tear escaped her wide blue eyes.

Very gently, Kane wiped that tear from her cheek, and in his strong arms, embraced Ridley in a hug that meant everything to them both. A long, silent minute passed, neither willing to break the spell, until at last Kane eased her away from him. Desperate to reveal the truth in his heart — a truth she had always known — but reluctant to say too much, he simply asked, "Alexandria Ridley... are you ready to explore the mausoleum of a fallen princess?"

A simple nod and a smile was a more than adequate answer for Kane and they wandered among the growing crowds along the narrow, beautiful twin reflection pools, the unmatched beauty of the Taj Mahal before them a veritable siren in the now golden light of an Indian dawn.

HIRAM KANE AND ALEXANDRIA RIDLEY were old friends from their university years back in England — the memories of which at times seemed like decades ago and at others like yesterday — and were on a well-earned holiday in India. Officially they were a relatively new couple, but the way they acted around each other meant that anyone who saw them together assumed they were a married couple — and if discovering they weren't, told them they should be.

They had shared many adventures together, some fun, others bordering on the suicidal, and remained trusted friends to this day. But despite Kane's best efforts, he'd never quite managed to convince Ridley they were indeed the perfectly compatible marriage-worthy couple. But Kane clung to the hope that this trip to India, especially coming so soon after their last, ill-fated adventure in the mountains of Peru, might be the time to sway the tide in his favour. And in his heart of hearts, Kane believed Alex was thinking along the same lines. He also believed that a dawn visit to the Taj Mahal, one of the most romantic destinations on the planet, certainly couldn't do his chances any harm.

A little over five hundred years ago fate shattered a Mughal emperor's heart. Shah Jahan's beautiful princess bride Mumtaz died suddenly in child birth, too young, and only a year into their happy marriage. It is said the Shah of Agra never got over the death of his alluring wife, but using his grief as inspiration he went on to build what many scholars agree is the most beautiful, artistically perfect manmade structure ever created.

The Taj Mahal was to become the princess's mausoleum, and for centuries since has been wowing tourists and visiting dignitaries with its symmetrical magnificence and dazzling artistry. Quite simply it remains one of mankind's most astonishing creations, and stands as both a testament to the love the Shah bestowed upon his young bride Mumtaz, and the ingenuity of what humans can create in the name of love and art.

Kane and Ridley walked quietly beside the serene reflection pools, the rising sun warming their faces and the vibrant yellows, pinks and reds of the ladies' saris coming alive in the magical morning light. The builders of the Taj itself used the purest white marble and, inlaid with millions of dazzling jewels and adorned with the delicate script of the Koran in a stylised, flowing font, it remains a veritable artistic masterpiece.

As inch by inch the sun rose, so the Taj began to glow. If a witness to its beauty didn't know of its earthly provenance, it would be easy to imagine its creators being otherworldly, such is its mystical power. Ridley couldn't keep her eyes from it. Kane witnessed the power of the Taj once before during a mid-nineties backpacking trip with his old friend Evan Craft. They too were bewitched by the Taj Mahal, and he had fond memories of witnessing all the reactions of those lucky others enough to behold the daily spectacle of magic that morning.

And now, as he glanced at Ridley, it was obvious she felt the same. They approached the first steps up onto the building's main platform, but he steered Ridley away from the swelling hordes of tourists, some in awe, others snapping selfies they would post once on Instagram, count the 'Likes', and never look at again. Kane never understood that new phenomenon and was dismayed at tourists who failed to appreciate the moment.

A hundred yards to the east of the main structure, and in the welcome shade of a large cypress tree, Kane pulled off his backpack and laid down a blanket upon which he set a small picnic hamper. It was still early, barely seven in the morning, but already the sun was beating down. From the hamper he pulled some breakfast things and, to Ridley's delight, a bottle of chilled champagne.

"What's the occasion?" she asked, but was well aware Kane didn't need one.

"Oh nothing," he said, "besides the fact we're alive, we're here in this wonderful place together and, well, why not?" It was a sound reason for Ridley, who enjoyed a breakfast mimosa as much as anyone. He handed her a glass and poured himself one, then Kane relaxed back on his elbows. "She's really something, isn't she?"

"Who's she?"

"The Taj. Obviously female. Nothing male could be as beautiful." Ridley got the humour, but Kane had a point. Throughout the history of art – and both Kane and Ridley considered the structure before them was artwork – people referred to inanimate objects such as boats, weapons, even countries, as male or female. Built for a beloved dead princess, the mausoleum had inspired literature and poems and architecture all around the world, and in that peaceful moment, as it was inspiring Ridley, she had to agree that the Taj was indeed female.

"It's visiting places like this I... well, I'm at my most... spiritual? I'm not really a spiritual person, as you kno –"

Kane almost choked on his mimosa. "Never a truer word spoken."

Ridley shot him an admonishing glance. "Ha! Very funny," she said, "but you get what I mean. It gets me questioning human nature, and what brings out the best in people. We've seen some of the very worst of humanity in recent times, right?"

Ridley was referring to the recent tragic events in Peru, which had resulted in several deaths, including children, and one of their closest friends. She continued.

"Sometimes it's just nice to experience the best of things, of people, humanity... and I was wondering..." Ridley had a sly look in her eyes Kane enjoyed. Amused, he suspected where this was heading.

"Yes? You were wondering?" Kane didn't worry. Whatever it was, he was certain it involved fun.

"Well, I know we planned to head south to the beach in Goa before heading north into the mountains. But..."

"But?"

"Well, how about we change plans and head north first instead?"

Kane shook his head, fighting hard to conceal his grin.

"You do remember why we're here, don't you?" she asked.

Of course he did, but he wouldn't let on. He frowned, and Ridley's heart sank.

She knew Hiram had his heart set on a little beach time, catching some sun and surf, perhaps even some scuba diving, but she hoped he'd like the idea, especially for such an important reason she couldn't believe he'd ignore. "Hiram, it's for Ev —" she started, but Kane cut her off.

"Come on, Alex," he said, "you know how much I want to hit the beach, slurping cocktails out of coconuts and eating my way through half the curry in India."

Ridley nodded slowly, defeated. She turned back to gaze upon the Taj.

"But, well... I guess someone might have the skills to persuade me." A trademark wry grin crept onto his face, and he lay back, shoved his hands behind his head, and closed his eyes.

Okay, now I get it. "Hmm, like that, is it?" Ridley purred, and slid into the crook of Kane's arm. "What can I do to change your mind?"

At that very moment a subtle cough made them sit up. A Taj Mahal groundsman walked nearby, a smile in his eyes on an otherwise deadpan face. He didn't look round, but he'd done the trick. They both guessed what he was thinking: get a room.

Embarrassed, Kane eased himself away from Alex. "Okay, it's a great idea," he said, smiling. "After all, there is some phenomenal hiking up in those hills."

Ridley jabbed Kane hard in his ribs, but understood he was teasing. Kane's best friend, Evan Craft, had tragically died the previous autumn while helping save the life of a young Quechuan man in Peru's Andes mountains. At the end of what was an unimaginable series of events, an earthquake spilled Kane and the boy over the edge of a mile-high cliff. Somehow, Kane had managed to arrest their fall by grabbing onto exposed tree roots, and the boy in turn clung onto Kane. With the help of Ridley, Professor John Onions and Evan, after a daring rescue they had managed to haul the boy to safety, more or less unharmed. They then hauled Kane to safety too, but in an unbelievable twist of cruel fate, Evan somehow toppled over the side of the cliff and plummeted to his death.

It was a horrific finale to what had been the worst episode of Kane's career. Despite accomplishing the main purpose of the expedition – finding the long lost Inca city of Vilcabamba, and with it the revered lost haul of Atahualpa's gold – Kane had lost his best friend. Aged just forty, Evan had died in the prime of his life.

Evan had been on many of Kane's expeditions, both official and otherwise. Journeying to Dharamshala to attend one of the Dalai Lama's monthly spiritual teachings was the single experiential bucket list item not yet scratched off. It's not that Evan was a spiritual man; like both Kane and Alex, he wasn't. But he had always admired what the much respected, almost secular Tibetan leader of all Buddhism stood for, and he wanted to experience the teachings for himself. In a cruel twist of irony, it was the acts of two separate religious terrorist factions – the Catholic Eagle Alliance and the pagan Inca Uprising – that had ultimately cost Evan his life. Only Evan himself might have seen the funny side of that particular irony. But soon after Evan's funeral Kane made a decision; that as soon as the chance arose, he would go himself to visit the Dalai Lama's Tsug-lag-khang Temple in Mcleodganj, and in honour of his friend, would listen to the words of His Holiness.

"And you never know, Hiram Kane, perhaps you might become enlightened."

Kane didn't flinch, so Ridley jabbed him again, snapping him back from his momentary melancholy.

"Huh? Ow. Oh, sorry… I was just thinking about Evan."

Ridley smiled. "I know you were. I

was just saying that even you might become enlightened."

Kane doubted that, though he had long admired the Dalai Lama. No, Hiram truly believed that if all the world took on board just some of the humanist lessons His Holiness taught, then it would become a much better place. And not just for Buddhists, either, but for everyone, no matter where they came from or what, if anything, they believed in.

Kane turned to face Ridley. His heart ached for the loss of his friend, but at the same time sensed it healing from the love he felt both for, and from, Alex. Everything would be alright. "Sure thing," he said. "Let's go up north early. For Evan."

"For Evan," she replied, smiling, and proffered her plastic cup of champagne.

Over the next half an hour they reminisced about their friend and finished off the now tepid bubbly, then packed up the accoutrements of their picnic and dumped the rubbish in a nearby bin.

Kane grabbed Ridley's hand and, joining the procession of tourists, led her towards the Taj.

"Thanks for agreeing to go to Dharamshala early," she said, and after a pause, added, "That's one of the... two... reasons I love you."

"Just two? I could name a doz —"

But before Kane could finish his sentence Ridley had slipped her hand from his and was soon dodging in and out of the throngs of wide-eyed tourists and pilgrims, eager to pay her respects to tragic Princess Mumtaz Mahal.

Kane again shook his head, always enamoured by Ridley's passion and enthusiasm. He smiled, took a deep breath, and looked up once more at the majesty of the Taj Mahal.

"This is going to be a good trip, Evan," he whispered, and made his way after Ridley.

But Hiram Kane had been wrong before.

Enjoy this sample of the latest Hiram Kane book?

Buy The Shadow of Kailash Now by typing this link into your browser:

https://geni.us/TheShadowOfKailashAMS

Turn the page for a taster of the next bestselling Hiram Kane book in the series, ***The Feathered Serpent.***

THE FEATHERED SAMPLE - A SAMPLE

PROLOGUE

Canãda de la Virgin, San Miguel de Allende, Mexico

Flames flickered from the rustic torches hung on the stone walls. Shadows danced wildly across those ancient stones, their haunting silence only heightening the child's terror. One shadow in particular leapt and danced, its wings jerking in crazed, untamed directions, though their owner stood statuesque before her, the gargoyle mask terrifying, his lack of communication even more so.

The girl, Rosa, had lost track of how long she'd been strapped to the cold stone plinth. A few hours? Days? It mattered little. Rosa was only nine-years-old, but somehow she knew what was to come. The creature... was it a man? The thing before her had said only a few words since they'd snatched her from outside her house.

"Un sacrifice digno," he'd whispered. *A worthy sacrifice.*

Rosa knew she was bright, though she definitely wasn't the smartest girl in her class. She wasn't even the brightest girl in her family... That was Flor, her younger sister. But she was smarter than Juanito, her fourteen-year-old brother. Rosa was glad Flor had gone to the store with Juanito when the man came and took her.

The torch flames flickered. The shadow wings danced.

And now the unsaid words echoed around her terrified mind...

Un sacrificio digno.

Un sacrificio digno.

Un sacrificio digno.

A worthy sacrifice.

ONE OF THOSE DAYS

Bonds 007 Bar, San Miguel de Allende, Mexico

Danny climbed the three flights of narrow stairs to what had become a kind of sanctuary for him over the last few months. The stairs took him up to a low-key James Bond themed bar in the city he had called home for the last couple of years: San Miguel de Allende, Mexico. The small, beautiful Spanish colonial-era city in central Mexico's high desert region had proven to be the perfect place in which to live a low-profile existence while still being surrounded by stunning art and architecture, and a perfect climate in what was known locally as the city of eternal spring. San Miguel had been recommended by a friend, Migdalia, and the city's beauty and peaceful atmosphere had bewitched him from the moment he first arrived.

"Hey buddy... the usual?" asked the bar owner, though he'd already begun pouring a gin.

"Yeah, thanks... make it a double."

"Double it is, coming right up." He poured the large gin and placed it before the man now sitting in his usual seat at the bar, then he stepped back and leaned on the counter. Bit early for a double, he thought.

"Everything alright, bud? You usually wait until afternoon before hitting the doubles. It's eleven-fifteen... wanna talk about it?"

The man looked up at Kenny Peters, the owner, who immediately knew everything was not okay with his friend.

"It's those dreams again, isn't it?"

Danny nodded, then offered the hint of a smile. It soon faded.

Kenny poured himself his preferred early drink, a little beer, which wasn't a beer at all, but a shot of the Mexican liquor, 43, and a splash of thick cream. Kenny had a distinct notion it was going to be one of those days.

He stepped from behind the bar and took the stool next to his friend. Though Kenny knew hardly anything about the man, they'd forged a pretty tight bond over the last few months. Kenny liked him for many reasons, not least the amount of money he spent in his bar. But more than that, the guy was quiet, thoughtful, never any trouble and, perhaps best of all, in a town full of people who had little better to do than whine about their lives and about getting old, especially the wealthy retired gringos and gringas from north of the border, and those out to make a quick buck or peso, whether by legitimate means or otherwise, this guy was honest.

"So, it's the dreams?"

"Yep. They're coming more and more often. Darker, too, and so real, Kenny. Almost as if it's reality, and not a dream at all. Except as always, it's not me that goes missing, it's... well, you know."

"You mean your brother?"

"Yes." The man never spoke of his brother directly, but occasionally referred to him in relation to other glimpses into his past.

Kenny didn't know the truth, and he would never ask. But from the bits and pieces he had learned, and short snippets and anecdotes Danny had revealed, usually when drunk, he gathered that his friend had left his native England a long time ago, and put simply, had been living in hiding ever since. He knew nothing more than that, other than sensing a deep regret in his friend, perhaps remorse, and he knew without doubt that a deeply troubled soul sat beside him at his bar that sunny Tuesday morning.

"Look, I know I suggested it before, but why don't you see a doctor? Maybe even a shrink? Get some help. Surely they can give you something, help you sleep a little better."

His friend glanced sideways at him then, and raised his gin. "Thanks Kenny. I appreciate your trust and friendship. But I know what I need to do. I've always known it. I just can't." A pause, then, "I never can."

Each man took a long gulp and finished their drinks at the same time. Kenny then stood and returned behind the bar to pour fresh ones. Once he'd sat down again, he asked, "You mean contact them? Your family in England?"

Danny nodded, then looked up, his brown/green eyes wet with emotion. "Yes, that's what I should do. Make contact. Tell them I'm sorry. Sorry for what I did, what I put them through. But... but it's been so long now..." There was a long pause. The man downed his new drink in one long gulp, then tuned to Kenny, hot tears now flowing unabashed.

"But I can't do that. I am sure now that they believe their grandson, son and brother is long dead. That Danny Kane is dead." He slammed the glass down on the bar, and added, "So Kenny, my friend, let's drink, and raise our glasses to the dead."

Kenny Peters sighed and stood up. He was right. It was definitely going to be one of those days.

Enjoy this sample of the latest Hiram Kane book?

Buy The Feathered Serpent Now by typing this link into your browser:

https://geni.us/FeatheredSerpent

Turn the page for a taster of the next bestselling Hiram Kane book in the series, ***Of Curses and Kings***.

OF CURSES AND KINGS - A SAMPLE

PROLOGUE

Alexandria, Egypt

Abbe Abidi

Abbe Abidi placed down his cup of mint tea and leaned back in his chair, gazing out across the railing of his balcony and squinting his brown eyes west against the dazzling orange sun as it dropped closer to the horizon far to his left. He scratched at his aquiline nose, an unconscious sign of nerves. Glancing at his small glass of tea, he grinned and shook his head. *Who the hell am I kidding?* He ducked back inside, poured himself a large scotch and downed it in one. Then he poured another and returned to his chair on the balcony.

His fancy apartment in the upmarket area off El-Gaish Road in western Alexandria overlooked popular Abo Haif Sidi Bisher Beach, where the passive waters of the Mediterranean Sea lapped constantly at its shore. The soothing sound of those gentle waves was often the soundtrack Abbe fell asleep to at night. Well that, and the constant accompaniment of beeping car horns and angry, shouting drivers on what was one of Egypt's busiest roads four storeys below his terrace. Half the reason he went to work so early every morning and left so late most evenings was to avoid the heavy traffic. Besides, it wasn't as if the director of the Alexandria International Museum had anything better to do than be at work anyway. Except drink. These days he always drank.

His beloved wife, Fatima, had died a couple of years ago, way too young. His children had flown the nest, both studying abroad and, sadly, not following in the academic footsteps he'd hoped they would. Abbe had a daughter studying science in Philadelphia and his son, his pride and joy, was following his passion for media in Berlin. Neither of them had said more than a dozen words to him in many months. Still, Abbe was proud of them both and was glad they'd taken more after their mother than him. *At least they're seeing the world,* he mused... *more than can be said for me these days.*

Abbe Abidi was a morose fifty-something who'd lost all passion for life after Fatima had died from cervical cancer a little over two years ago. She had always been his shining light, especially since the kids had left for far-flung universities a few years back. After studying antiquities for the best part of four decades, he knew that without Fatima he was turning into an antiquity himself.

He finished the scotch in two gulps, then stood up, his bland clothes hanging looser on his already slender frame in recent months. He took a last glance at the sun as it finally dipped beyond the horizon, then stepped through the French doors, closed them to shut off the incessant noise from below, and returned to his study. Abbe almost always felt a sense of comfort in his study, surrounded by a collection of academic books three decades in the making, several of which he'd authored himself. It was his quiet zone, somewhere to think clearly and forget about what he'd lost since Fatima had passed away. It was his sanctuary.

Abbe caught a glimpse of himself in a mirror as he stood beside his desk. His dark hair was fading to grey at the sides... *I'm sure I'm greyer than I was this morning,* he thought... and it was thinning rapidly, though that was a trait he'd inherited from his father, the former director of the museum, and a man famous across Egypt in their particular corner of the academic world. Adil Abidi was a man — *the* man — who'd campaigned vehemently for the Egyptian antiquities department to push for museums around the world to begin repatriating Egypt's lost artefacts. He wouldn't say lost. He'd say stolen. When he had died a decade ago, he'd left not only a large void in the Abidi family, but large boots to fill at the Alexandria International Museum, boots Abbe had been trying his utmost to fill ever since he'd stepped into the role of director. Whether he'd succeeded or not would ultimately for others to decide. The events that would occur over the course of the next few weeks would also play a major factor in securing his much-desired legacy.

Yet, Abbe's office didn't feel like a relaxing sanctuary this evening. Tonight he was to participate in a four-way conference call with three other men, two of whom he'd never met and knew nothing about, other than their supposed roles in the endeavour about to get underway a few weeks from now. Abbe Abidi was nervous. He'd run through how he expected the conversation to go in his mind a dozen times already, and still he couldn't shake the feeling that he was making a terrible mistake. But Abbe was invested now. Whatever he did in the next fortnight, whatever choices he made, whether to continue on the path he was on, or to back the hell out, the director felt certain that his life, such as it was, would never be the same again.

He took a seat in his ancient leather chair at an equally ancient desk and slipped open a draw. He grabbed out a small plastic bottle and snapped off the lid. He threw back two of the painkillers to stave off the pounding headache that had come on suddenly, then threw back two more just to be sure. He washed them down with a long gulp of a freshly poured scotch. Next he checked his watch. 8:45 P.M.

After a long, deep inhale, Abbe closed his eyes and prayed his headache would go before the conference call went live in fifteen minutes.

If he answered the call, Abbe knew there was definitely no turning back.

If he didn't answer it, he equally knew there would be nowhere to hide.

Salam al Halabi

London, England

Salam al Halabi needed to end the call.

"Sure thing, of course. Okay, I've got to run. I'll see you at work tomorrow."

Salam al Halabi stashed his phone and swiftly descended into the London Underground at Holborn. Twenty minutes later he emerged into a warm evening at bustling Liverpool Street Station, then made the short walk to his modest one-bedroom flat in Shoreditch. It had been a long, busy but ultimately good day at work, yet for the last hour or two Salam's nerves had started to get the better of him. He'd just called his friend, Aleesha — where they dating? He wasn't quite sure — because he'd missed her at work and hadn't had time for their usual pint once they'd left The British Museum, where they both worked as assistant curators.

He hadn't had time for that pint, because time was seriously ticking for Salam.

The twenty-five year old hated when he got kept behind after hours for one inane meeting or another. Although Salam loved his job as assistant curator, these meetings were almost always a waste of time. This one had been no exception. And this evening, time was something Salam had very little of. In just half an hour, at 8:00 P.M. GMT, Salam was to take part in a conference call that would almost certainly change his life.

He kicked off his shoes and fired up his MacBook, then slumped down onto his bony couch. The BBC News reporter on TV was droning some shit or other about the prime minister once more embarrassing himself — which Salam believed the blonde buffoon did every time he opened his mouth — and he hit mute on the remote. The flat was cosy and quiet, despite the busy high street just below his first-floor window, and he'd made it as homely as possible on his assistant's salary. Salam felt he'd been overlooked far too long for a promotion at the British Museum, which severely pissed him off. Nevertheless, he worked hard and with diligence. He knew he was up against it. Racial tensions had grown in the last couple of years, as much of Europe seemed to be taking a more conservative, right-wing angle, and as a British Muslim of Egyptian descent, Salam knew there were likely to be even tougher times ahead.

Salam ran a hand though his thick black hair, then adjusted his glasses. He glanced at the digital clock on the TV. 7:58 P.M. Almost time for the call. Salam's throat suddenly felt dry, and he hustled to refill his water cup in the kitchen, catching a glimpse of the Brick Lane mosque through the window. Feeling a little calmer having seen the mosque, he returned to the sofa and placed his MacBook on his lap. One more minute.

Jabari Nader

Cairo, Egypt

Jabari Nader glanced at the clock on the wall of the gym. 8:40 P.M. Five more minutes, then I'll go.

He pumped the hefty weights, twenty-two pound dumbbells, slowly and repeatedly for exactly five more minutes, then placed them down at his feet. He grunted a farewell at a couple of friends struggling beneath gargantuan barbells, then left the gym. He climbed onto his powerful motorbike and screeched away to his flat several blocks along the road. Taking the stairs two at a time for three full flights, his muscle-bound legs powering him upwards, Jabari entered the expansive flat and grabbed a huge carton of orange juice from the fridge. He downed half of it in one go.

Then he stepped into the shower and rinsed away the sweat beneath the cold water. Once he had finally cooled off, he draped a large white towel around his powerful body, admiring himself in the full length mirror as he walked into the lounge, then took a seat behind his desk. He checked the time on his monitor. 8:57 P.M. Perfect. Biting into a large apple, Jabari sat back and waited for the conference call to start, a grin creeping across his handsome face.

With a shaved head and hard eyes, Jabari looked like someone who knew how to handle himself. And the man didn't disappoint. After retiring from the Egyptian Special Forces a decade previous, the then thirty-five year old had set up his own private security firm, catering to all kinds of people, from government officials, to actors and singers, and occasionally even Egyptian royalty. However, Jabari had recently been approached for a one-off gig. After turning down it down several times, for a variety of reasons, not least the fact that it sounded completely impossible, he had finally been made an offer he simply couldn't refuse.

Jabari was told the overall gist of the assignment by a man named Bassam. But in a couple of minutes' time he'd be speaking to Bassam's boss, the financier of the project. The mastermind of the gig. That man would also be on the call, as well as another man. The mastermind would inform Jabari and the others of the plan's finer details. Jabari had been promised it was to be the job of a lifetime, and as he thought of the massive financial rewards he'd been assured, his grin spread just that little bit wider.

Omar Abdel-Rahman

Paris, France

Omar Abdel-Rahman glanced up as his butler knocked twice and entered the room.

"It is almost time for your call, sir," said the diminutive servant Bassam in his exquisitely manicured English accent. "Are you ready?"

"Yes, thank you Bassam. That will be all," Omar replied in his even more refined accent, clipped to within an inch of its life in the dusty halls of Cambridge in the sixties and as perfect now as it was then. Back then he'd used his charm to talk his way into the high society of British academia, hobnobbing with such leading archaeological lights as Jacquetta Hawkes, Thomas Charles Lethbridge and Sir Leonard Woolley.

Bassam silently left his boss's penthouse suite, an opulent space that occupied the entire top floor of the apartment block nestled in one of the most expensive bits of real estate in the world, Avenue Émile-Deschanel, in the 7th Arrondissement, Paris. Not that price mattered to Omar Abdel-Rahman, one of the wealthiest men in all Egypt. Omar had an oversized personality that matched his rotund physique, and a jovial voice that boomed with confidence. His jet black, shiny and coiffured hair added a certain elegance to his appearance, though the out-of-place pencil moustache detracted from what some considered a handsome, if not bloated face. His

Armani suit cost more than the average Egyptian's annual income, yet despite his wealth and extravagant lifestyle, Omar was considered — by others as well as by himself — a man of the people. He had put millions of his own fortune into a range of charities, and was never one to turn down an invite to celebrity charitable events, where the champagne flowed, and his philanthropic reputation continued to thrive, much like his impressive waistline.

Omar had amassed his personal fortune from the oil industry in the eighties, and though technically retired, his investments still brought in millions of dollars annually, most of which he spent on his one true passion in life; collecting priceless archaeological artefacts.

Such was the extent of his world-class collection, most of which was secured in his private museum on the floor directly beneath the penthouse suite, that Omar often loaned selections from it to exhibits all around the world. He was unabashedly proud of his collection, and it gave him immense satisfaction. But having the artefacts in his possession was one thing. It was the hunting down and attaining of those supposedly 'unattainable' artefacts that really got Omar's juices flowing.

One such item above all others kept Omar up at nights, more than any glamorous young suitor could, female or male. Omar had fended off almost as many of both as he'd entertained.

The particular artefact he had firmly in his sights now had been discovered by French soldiers in his Egyptian homeland in 1799, and not long after had been sold to the highest bidder. Thus it has remained in its current home for over two-hundred years; The British Museum.

And if flamboyant Omar Abdel-Rahman knew one thing about ancient archaeological artefacts, it's that they should always come home.

The Conference Call

The four men sat at four separate locations across Europe and Egypt, in two different time zones, each waiting in anticipation of the imminent conference call. Two of the men were nervous, as well as being undeniably excited. Another of them was ambivalent to the actual job — it was just that, a job — yet he couldn't help but wonder about how his life would change if they achieved success. The last of them was exhilarated that finally, his long-held dream — more a burning desire — was about to commence.

Thus, despite their four very different reasons for becoming involved in the imminent drama, all four men sat by their computers with baited breath, for a conversation that might very well be the defining moment of each of their respective lives.

Omar Abdel-Rahman leaned forward and pressed a button on his computer mouse, then stood up and turned to face a bank of monitors mounted to a wall, a large bay window offering a view of the Eiffel Tower just two-hundred and fifty yards to the north west.

One by one, three of the screens pinged to life in the Zoom app, each occupied by a different face.

Omar spread his arms wide, his huge grin almost matching it. "Good evening, gentlemen," he said, "and welcome to the first day of the rest of your lives. Inshallah."

THE KANE ESTATE, ENGLAND

Hiram Kane lay in a coma.

Well, to any observer it would have seemed like that. He lay on his front, his face wedged down into the soft cushion of the sun lounger, an unfortunate dribble of saliva dampening his chin. He wasn't aware of it, but if he did know he wouldn't have cared. It spoke of the tranquility he felt, the safety of his surroundings... the distance he currently was from things and people that could kill him and wanted to.

He had hardly moved in hours — days, in fact — and it was exactly what he needed. June this year was especially warm, and he was taking a hard-earned break from... Well, from everything. His body needed it, that was for sure. He still felt the aches and pains from a month ago, still wore the scars, and relished the opportunity for stillness. But more than his physical need for rest, his mind needed to recuperate. To recover.

He had just returned from a trip to Mexico, where he had been reunited with his long-lost brother Danny, who for close to three decades he had feared was dead. It was only after receiving an anonymous letter in the post that, for the first time in all those years, there was a glimmer of hope that he was alive.

He and his partner, Alexandria Ridley, had flown to Mexico immediately. The anonymous source of the letter, who they later learned was a man named Kenny Peters, had been right. Danny was indeed alive, in good health, and living a quiet life in the beautiful mountain town of San Miguel de Allende, in the central Mexican highlands.

The trip had turned out to be anything but the relaxing family reunion it was meant to be. As always, they'd found themselves inadvertently caught up in a horrendous episode, one during which a deranged professor risked the lives of dozens of innocent children. Somehow, Hiram and his friends survived the crazed archaeologist, who called himself Quetzal in reference to Quetzalcoatl, The Feathered Serpent, creator or life in almost all Meso-American cultures. The madman did kill two of his victims, and severely injured several others before Kane helped put an end to the madness.

The traumatising experiences of Mexico had left

deep mental scars for them all, and in a coordinated effort not to end up on any more crazy adventures, at least not any time soon, they'd holed up at Kane's grandparent's house in the English countryside, just on the border between rural Norfolk and Suffolk.

The Kane estate could not have been a more relaxed place to find some kind of normality again after the tribulations of the last couple of months, and indeed, several years. With the early summer sun beating down, and a beautiful outdoor pool to laze around, it was the proverbial heaven on Earth. So a little dribbling right now was just fine with Hiram Kane.

Hiram stirred at the sound of a splash in the nearby pool. He rolled over, propping himself on an elbow just in time to see Alex surface at the far end of the pool, turn, then continue powering across the pool's surface with one graceful stroke after another, her strong arms cutting through the water with apparent ease.

For so many years Hiram had loved Alex Ridley. They had shared many moments together over the last fifteen plus years since they'd met, and such was their affection for one another, most people who met them assumed they were a couple. But for reasons known only to her, Alex had always held back from making a firm commitment to Hiram, despite his best efforts. The fact that in her own way she had always loved him too was an awkward reality she did her best to deal with in silence.

After recent demoralising events, both alongside Hiram and on her own secret missions, Alex had come to realise just what a scary and dangerous place the world really was. Quite simply, there were too many people doing too many bad things to one another, and for reasons that could never, ever be justified.

In Hiram Kane, Alex had always known a different kind of man, a better kind, someone who always put others before himself, often to his own detriment. He was a man who had always seen the best in people, even if the evidence suggested they didn't deserve such trust. Despite his sharp intelligence, Kane was a simple man, an honest man with a heart so big there was room in it for everyone. Alex trusted Hiram Kane implicitly. She had always loved him, yet had kept her distance for only one reason: she hadn't been able to trust, nor could she love, herself.

There were some things Alex had been involved in recently, more recently even than their travails in India and Tibet, that Hiram didn't know of. She had grown stronger exponentially in the last months, so much so Alex had started to believe in herself again. She had seen things — done things — that would haunt her always, yet they were things that needed doing. And she had done them without hesitation.

Thus, Alex was a changed woman, now fulfilling the potential to be what Hiram had always told her she was; a good and positive force in the world. She'd resisted that notion most of her life, dismissed it as the ravings of a delusional man. But she now knew what she was capable of. She had made some decisions and taken decisive actions lately that had improved the lives — often saving them — of many desperate individuals, and removed from their lives the evil forces that sought to do them harm, or worse.

And now she had discovered her own light, there was no other person on Earth with whom she would rather share her best self with than Hiram Kane.

They'd met almost two decades ago on a taekwon-do sparring mat at university, and after she'd kicked Hiram's arse she'd invited him for a drink. They'd been each others' favourite human ever since that day, and whilst they'd never officially been a couple, they had always shared a unique and powerful kind of love.

Alex finally slipped out of the pool after a swift ten lengths, and let the water drip from her lithe body as she walked over towards Hiram.

"Hello, handsome," she said. "How was the nap? No doubt you were dreaming of me," she teased.

"No doubt about it," Hiram replied. "Any who wouldn't? You're a gorgeous woman, Alexandria Ridley." He grinned, the smile returned in kind by Alex.

"You should cut back on the compliments... might just give this girl a complex."

"Get you a drink?" he asked.

"Sure thing. Wine, thanks."

"Be right back." Hiram stood from his sun bed, his athletic frame browning nicely after several days slouched in the sun. His body was more or less recovered, and although they didn't discuss it often, his mind was close to healing too. The memories would always remain, bearing testament to the good people that had died in Mexico last month, and the many before that around the world. But Hiram had made an important decision in the last couple of weeks — probably the most important of his life — and now it was made there was no point sitting around feeling sorry for themselves any more. Life was short; Hiram and Alex knew that better than most.

It was time to move on.

On bare feet Hiram trotted to the nearby annex where a large fridge kept a generous stash of beer, wine and champagne nicely chilled. It was also where he had his phone on charge, and scooping it up from the table he saw there had been a missed call. He recognised the number and knew whose call he'd missed. It was a call they had been expecting, though not until next week. But it didn't matter. When he called back, it would be to have a conversation that would change everything.

Returning that call could wait for now. Taking the drink to Alex could not.

"M'lady," he said as he approached the love of his life. "One glass of sauvignon blanc."

"Why, thank you," she purred, taking the glass and savouring the crisp tartness of Oyster Bay, her favourite wine from the Marlborough region of New Zealand. After a second sip, she sighed with pleasure. "That is so good, thanks."

"And you're so welcome." He had to tell her. "So... I had a missed call." He gazed at Alex now, waiting for her reaction.

"Was it from who I think it was?"

"Yes, I believe so."

"Are you going to call back? I mean, it's important, right?"

Hiram didn't answer for a long moment, his eyes drifting from Alex to the huge stand of English oak trees bordering the property. He remained silent too, as if waiting for the right words to come. Finally, he turned his gaze back to Alex. "Yes, it's important, though the call can wait until tomorrow. But..."

"But what?"

"Well... I know we've already made the decision. But..."

"But what, Hiram? It's an amazing opportunity, right? I think it's just what you need. What we need." She reached out and took his hand in hers. "And you're the perfect person for the job, I know that."

Hiram nodded, the hint of a smile curling his lips. "You're right," he said. "So, we'd better pack our bags. We're going to Egypt."

Enjoy this sample of the latest Hiram Kane book?

Buy Of Curses and Kings Now by typing this link into your web browser:

https://geni.us/CursesandKingsAMS

Turn the page to sign up to my spam-free bi-weekly newsletter.

SIGN UP?

SIGN UP for my bi-weekly spam-free newsletter to keep up with all my new releases and future promotions, not to mention your chance to win signed copies.

Just type this link into your web browser:

www.subscribepage.com/stevenmooreauthor

AUTHOR'S NOTE

Hello there, Steven here.

Thanks for reading ***SILENT KNIGHT***

I often get asked where my story ideas emanate from. The simple answer? From my extensive travels and wonderful experiences around the world.

I first left my home country of England aged nineteen, and I've been travelling ever since — that's almost three decades... sshhh. I'm fortunate to have visited 60+ countries, worked on 4 continents, and I've met the most inspiring people. Combine this with real world events, historical characters, exotic locations, current social issues, my own interests and passions, and a large slice of imagination... and I have some pretty motivating material.

I actually live in San Miguel de Allende, Mexico most of the time, with my writer wife Leslie, and our two cats, Ernest Hemingway & F. Scott Fitzgerald

(Ernie & Fitz), and our rescue puppy, Charles Dickens. This means exciting settings and adventures are never far away... and we certainly seek them out.

Thanks so much for taking a chance on this book. If this is your first venture into Hiram Kane's world, I for one hope you'll stick around with us for the rest of the series (when he's in his thirties, and altogether a lot cooler than he was in this story). Things really kick off in The Tiger Temple and The Samurai Code... maybe check those out next (there are excerpts of the whole series below).

I also hope you'll check out all my other best-selling action/thriller/apocalyptic & literary novels.

If not, I might just send Ernie, Fitz and Dickens after you.

Cheers,

Steven

First published by **Condor Publishing** in 2020

Printed in Great Britain
by Amazon

84345345R00180